ALSO BY JONAS LÜSCHER

Barbarian Spring

kraft

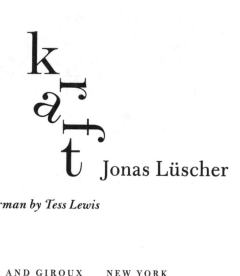

k r a f t

Jonas Lüscher

Translated from the German by Tess Lewis

FARRAR, STRAUS AND GIROUX   NEW YORK

Fiction
Lüscher,
J

Farrar, Straus and Giroux
120 Broadway, New York 10271

Printed in the United States of America
Originally published in German in 2017 by Verlag C.H. Beck, Germany
English translation published in the United States by Farrar, Straus and Giroux
First American edition, 2020

Library of Congress Cataloging-in-Publication Data
Names: Lüscher, Jonas, 1976– author. | Lewis, Tess, translator.
Title: Kraft / Jonas Lüscher ; translated from the German by Tess Lewis. Other
  titles: Kraft. English
Description: First American edition. | New York : Farrar, Straus and Giroux,
  2020. | Originally published in German in 2017 by Verlag C.H. Beck,
  Germany. | Includes bibliographical references.
Identifiers: LCCN 2020023952 | ISBN 9780374182144 (hardcover)
Classification: LCC PT2712.U87 K7313 2020 | DDC 833/.92—dc23
LC record available at https://lccn.loc.gov/2020023952

Designed by Richard Oriolo

Our books may be purchased in bulk for promotional, educational, or business
use. Please contact your local bookseller or the Macmillan Corporate and
Premium Sales Department at 1-800-221-7945, extension 5442, or by e-mail at
MacmillanSpecialMarkets@macmillan.com.

www.fsgbooks.com
www.twitter.com/fsgbooks • www.facebook.com/fsgbooks

10   9   8   7   6   5   4   3   2   1

The translation of this work received support from the Swiss Arts Council
Pro Helvetia.

swiss arts council
pr☐helvetia

kraft

chapter one

We've all been drawn into someone's love only to
find out that we couldn't afford it.

—PAUL FORD

rumsfeld's portrait hangs directly in Kraft's line of sight. When he finds himself stuck yet again, staring blankly into the void over the top of his computer screen, the portrait hovers like a blurry red, blue, and gray stain in front of the oak-paneled wall. It always takes a few breaths before the former secretary of defense's cold eyes behind rimless glasses reclaim their rights and, emitting a kind of guide beam, take control of Kraft's consciousness and force him to focus against his will until, in a single swift, fluid movement, the patches of color solidify into a concrete image and the nasolabial folds emerge, along with the thin, lipless mouth, the rather short nose—not exactly suited to the long-serving veteran hawk's notoriously caustic expression—the accurately combed silver hair, the precisely knotted tie that tightly grips the chicken neck and, with the assistance of the heavily starched shirt collar, prevents the scornful, self-confident face from escaping the pinstriped cloth and rising on the eagle wings outspread from the folds of the sky-blue banner behind this renowned aphorist's right ear before disappearing into loftier realms.

Just you wait, Kraft thought on his seventh day of sitting idly under this surveillance, torn once again from his vacuous thoughts by the imperious, demanding gaze, like it or not, I'm going to find a European tone. That's my plan. A European tone that will combine Leibniz's optimism and Kant's rigor with Voltaire's derisive scorn and Rabelais's irrepressible laughter and will unite them all in Hölderlinian spheres with Zola's sensitivity to human suffering and Mann's irony . . . no, better leave Mann out of it, that half Californian.

at first Kraft had taken it for a joke, six months earlier, when he'd opened Ivan's e-mail from Stanford with *Theodicy* in the subject line. But Ivan wasn't one for joking, never had been, not even back when they first met in Berlin in '81, and their regular correspondence over the decades since showed, in all its sober practicality, that neither the passing years nor the California sunshine had changed Ivan at all in that respect. The e-mail opened with *Dear Dick*, an English salutation Richard Kraft had gotten used to long before, just as he'd gotten used to the *Ivan* with which István Pánczél had at some point begun signing his communications—about the same time that brief e-mails began replacing letters typed on thin blue airmail paper. Ivan's e-mail continued: *We very much hope you will participate. We will cover all costs. Give my regards to Heike and the twins. Best, Ivan.*

In an attachment, Kraft found the lavishly designed call to enter the essay competition held in honor of the 307th anniversary of the publication of Leibniz's *Theodicy: Essays on the Goodness of God, the Freedom of Man, and the Origin of Evil*. The essay was to be on a subject based on the prize question set by the Prussian Academy of Sciences in 1753—"An examination of the system of Pope as it is contained in the dictum: 'Whatever is, is right,'"—albeit in a rather more streamlined but also more optimistic formulation:

THEODICY AND TECHNODICY:

OPTIMISM FOR A YOUNG MILLENNIUM:

Why whatever is, is right and why we still can improve it.

The modus operandi was clearly set out. All the submissions would be presented over the course of a single afternoon in Stanford University's CEMEX Auditorium. The essays would be read aloud one after the other in swift succession with a strictly enforced eighteen-minute time limit; the use of presentation software was strongly encouraged; a select and illustrious audience would be in attendance; and the world—the organizers seemed confident of the world's interest—would be tuned in via livestream. The author of the winning essay would receive one million dollars.

Yes, indeed, Kraft thought, at that price, one can certainly be confident of catching the world's attention.

efore reading further, his eyes lingered for a moment on the oddly boyish face of a man in his best years. *Tobias Erkner, Entrepreneur, Investor, and Founder of the Amazing Future Fund*, the caption said of the flat-nosed man with a flashbulb's ring-shaped reflection in his irises, which conjured up a gleam of youthful enthusiasm in the otherwise expressionless eyes. Kraft couldn't remember ever having read a text that defied reason as blatantly as the one in which the aforementioned Tobias Erkner presented his vision under his own portrait and explained why it was so terribly urgent for the best and the brightest around the world to take up this question, along with his motivation for underwriting the reward with a million dollars of his private fortune.

Not that Kraft was unacquainted with texts in which the oddest ideas in intellectual history were justified with the crudest of convictions. He had seen his share from a certain kind of intelligent first-year student who had read too many of the wrong books too early, which could, when combined with a particular hormonal disposition, lead to volatile situations. In general, he was able to iron out such wrinkles in a semester or two.

But this here was something different. With apparent effortlessness and an irresistible matter-of-factness, the founder of the Amazing Future Fund was able to establish what seemed like perfectly logical connections between obviously false statements, contradictory notions, and things that clearly had nothing to do with each other. What Kraft found most disturbing was the complete absence of emphatic rhetoric. Erkner's language was crystal clear, straightforward, and free of any attempt to take the reader's emotions hostage. It would have been easy to diagram the arguments logically, to transform Erkner's text into a column of predicators and logical connectives, at the bottom of which his conclusion would ineluctably and necessarily stand, even if, as was clear to Kraft, every one of the premises was false. But that seemed to be of no interest to the author as long as the formal rules of language were followed. Kraft was appalled.

Unfortunately, he was not able to replicate Erkner's rigor when he tried to explain to Heike why he had to leave her alone with the twins for four weeks in September. She had laughed and, abashed, he had stared down at her large bare feet and polished toenails.

f inding the right tone, whether a European one as he has envisioned or any other, is proving difficult for Kraft because a muffled roar and furious howling are echoing everywhere and at nearly all hours throughout the rooms of the Hoover Institution on War, Revolution, and Peace. A droning and hissing escape from an antiquated stainless-steel casing that sits like a jet pack on the back of a hefty Mexican woman, so that Kraft occasionally indulges in the fancy that her corpulence alone keeps her from blasting off and is the reason why the appliance so audibly strains at the limits of its powers with a roar that swells and ebbs to the rhythm of the greedy nozzle the woman stoically pushes over the carpet. There always seems to be something to vacuum up in the Hoover Institution on War, Revolution, and Peace.

If Kraft didn't feel quite so overwhelmed by the task facing him, perhaps the former secretary of defense's expression would seem less scornful and the drone of the vacuum cleaner less deafening and he would be able to ignore both, but as it is he has no option but to regularly flee the smug hawk and the woman's snarling appliance and seek refuge on the fourteenth floor of this tower bursting with books on war, revolution, and peace in the hope that it was still too early for any large flocks of Asian tourists to interrupt his contemplation and spoil his enjoyment of the view.

On the observation platform, Kraft settles into one of the tall grille-fronted niches and stares out past the rough-hewn ornamentation so well suited to the brutish proportions of the tower, which appears from a distance to be built of a single block but, seen from up close, reveals a peculiar sandy surface texture that makes it look like it's part of a stage set. Kraft's gaze flits impatiently over the campus landscape of red-tiled roofs spread out at his feet and disdainfully appraises the whole of Silicon Valley: What does he care about this mystical valley, this seething mass of buildings with its strange cults and places of worship, cradle of this or that digital life-form? It's not his religion. He rests his eyes on the hazy city skyline to the north and searches his heart for a sense of regret.

Kraft is alone in his contempt. As a rule, the tower sends other visitors into ecstasies. They leap excitedly back and forth between the photographs of the surroundings hung on the columns and adorned with small arrows and captions drawing attention to the local attractions and views visible behind the grilles. They point out this or that building complex, accompanying the entire hubbub with polyphonic cries of admiration and detailed explanations in languages Kraft does not understand except for a few expressions they seem to shout into the blue Californian sky with particular emphasis and enthusiasm as if these were names of gods and saints they were compelled to invoke. *There, there,* one seems to be calling, his index finger indicating a spot to the north not far from the campus, *Facebook!* Awed cries of recognition rise in chorus and everyone's eyes follow the extended finger. Another points in the direction of the bay with an exclamation, of which Kraft only catches *Google,* that is met with ardent cries and intensive searching until a young man draws the group's attention away with a shout of *Hewlett Packard*, and they all rush to the north side of the tower while someone else waves toward the south, curving his hand in a gesture to indicate the other side of the mountain. *Cupertino*, he says reverently. *Ahhh, Cupertino, Apple*, they intone in response and chant the sainted name several times as they take pictures with telephoto lenses of the hill behind which the conjured fruit lies hidden.

Although he finds it all immensely irritating, Kraft forbids himself to think in terms of *the West* or of *decline*, but instead turns obstinately toward the carillon that stands completely neglected in the middle of the space open to the weather on all sides, its console enclosed in a small glass cubicle, the bells hanging from the beams overhead. Unsolicited, one of the Hoover Institution's red-jacketed elevator men had informed Kraft about every detail of the unusual instrument. The number of bells: forty-eight. The inscription on the largest bell: *For Peace Alone Do I Ring*. The extreme difficulty of playing the instrument: only one professor in the entire Music Department—the last of his kind, so to speak—can do it. Kraft knows this isn't true. But what an enticing thought that is, he thinks, how enticing and utterly laughable it would be if he were the very last person in the entire world who knew how to play this exceptional instrument. He pictures himself sitting on the bench in the small glass cubicle banging his fists on the batons of the keyboard and pressing the pedals with his feet to make the large bells peal. He'd give them what for. You'd hear it throughout the entire valley. Maybe even as far as the city in the fog if he stomped hard enough on the lowest pedal. Would she hear it? Johanna, whom he'd so infuriated thirty years ago that she had disappeared to San Francisco forever. *For Peace Alone Do I Ring*.

eike had let out a laugh, short and sharp. Then she'd shrewdly picked apart Erkner's text, and done so with such apparent ease, in fact, that Kraft was no longer sure why it had made a deep impression on him, why he'd been so appalled. Furious, he tore from her hand the paper on which he had printed out the essay question, leaving a stinging paper cut on her index finger.

he night before he left, they had argued.

Exhausted, they waited at the crack of dawn for Kraft's taxi to the airport. Heike stood in the doorway, tall, blond, barefoot again, and Kraft's eyes were caught for an absurdly long time by her bunions, those inflamed, bony protuberances that struck him as the manifestation of their relationship's pathology. He fussed with his suitcase's telescopic handle. Go, win, and come back with the prize money so we can all have our freedom again, she said. Kraft searched in vain for a sarcastic undertone to her words. He felt a sudden impulse to give her a hug and set his bag aside, but Heike had already closed the door.

raft spent his hours in flight using every meteorological phenomenon and every geographic feature as grounds for cultivating his faint melancholy into a pathos-drenched catharsis. From the deserted streets in the dawning light to the rain-soaked runway, from the clouds over the North Sea and Ireland's green fields, across the endless expanse of the Atlantic—which, admittedly, he'd slept through—to Greenland's dazzling ice sheet, agleam below him in inapposite sunlight, he worked himself into a fit of self-pitying grief over the breakdown of his marriage, which suddenly struck him as inevitable, and following a vague sense of duty, he heroically reviewed the good moments they'd shared, beginning with their first encounter at a meeting of the university's administrative reform board, which Heike was attending as the representative of a management consulting firm and during which she had managed, with a furious round of PowerPoint slides of pie-chart and bar diagrams, to antagonize the entire group of professors twice her age, with the exception of him, Richard Kraft, who threw himself into the breach for her and her diagrams out of a fundamental instinct of dissidence and in provocatively expressed affirmation of the principles of economic liberalism—a provocation that didn't have the slightest effect on his colleagues, who ignored his sallies as routinely as he presented them, as if his provocations were a threadbare and rather stained rug that had been left in the wrong place in the wrong room and had a tendency in moments of inattention—in other words, regularly—to raise its fringed edges, a daily hindrance, but not one worth getting agitated about. But perhaps he was also following an initial surge of spontaneous infatuation, a gesture for which Heike showed her appreciation by praising, in front of his colleagues, his open-mindedness toward her methodology before pointing out that he had drawn completely erroneous conclusions from her tables and figures and that his calculations were off by two decimal points.

Then he conjured up his first invitation, which she had finally accepted after some initial hesitation and which involved his attempt to impress her by serving up a buffet of prominent acquaintances from Tübingen's academic circles and a sauerbraten with handmade spätzle. This attempt, it turned out, was successful since Heike had offered to stay on after the guests had left at a late hour and help him with the washing up, an effort abandoned halfway through, interrupted as it was by the conception of their twin girls, whose birth and first few birthdays Kraft now reviewed, a glass of tomato juice in hand ten thousand meters over the ice sheet, and by the time he reached his daughters' third birthday the feeling crept over him that in the last fourteen years he had never had the chance to complete that half-finished washing up, so powerfully had the needs of his young wife and daughters encroached on his life, already overflowing with teaching and administrative duties, the pressure to publish, and the thirst for recognition, leading Kraft to the conclusion that his second marriage was not suited to helping him forget the failure of his first.

maybe a European tone isn't such a good idea after all. He has to be pragmatic and in this case that means being optimistic. Just this once. Not that he finds it easy or has the feeling that he—or the rest of the world—has any reason to be optimistic. Quite the contrary. But he knows what's expected of him. In any case, it's a matter of convincing a jury. A jury and the donor, who, not unwisely, has reserved the final decision for himself. One million. All of his problems solved in one fell swoop. No, Kraft knows that's not really true. But at least it would allow him to concentrate on his failure as a human being. Relieved of all earthly cares, he could devote himself to plumbing the depths of his own inadequacies. For this he could force himself to be optimistic, at least once. Whatever is, is right. It shouldn't be hard to come up with a few persuasive arguments in support of this proposition. At one point or another in history. Without heavy-handedly and predictably invoking the world spirit and calling on history itself as witness—Kraft is sure that Piet van Baasen and probably Sakaguchi too will take precisely this line. No, he has to come up with something original. World spirit. That ultimately amounts to saying, *Whatever is, will be right*. But when? As a matter of fact, Sakaguchi has already ridden that horse too far: confidently declaring that the time had come, and then finding himself forced to publicly recant like a prophet of the apocalypse on the morning after. No, what's required here is a more authentic, more contemporary optimism, that is, an active and effective optimism. No *Whatever is, will be right*, and definitely no *Whatever is, is bad* or *Whatever is, will become even worse*. For a million dollars, one has the right to expect a *Whatever is, is right*. And it's up to him to find the arguments to prove it.

But Kraft is having a hard time. And as always when he's having difficulties, he escapes into research.

but why is Kraft having such a hard time? You could say that it's complicated. It has to do with a convergence of the most disparate circumstances, all of them difficult to assess, especially for Kraft. And certain circumstances, internal and external, may be exerting a not inconsiderable amount of pressure, which is not exactly conducive to incisive thought. Or we could take the trouble to analyze the situation a bit and extract a short list from the muddle that would, in decreasing order of urgency, spell out the reasons why Kraft is unable to write:

1. The difficulty of the task itself
2. Kraft's inability to get over his jet lag
3. Kraft's family situation
4. Kraft's financial situation
5. The existential necessity of impressing the jury as a consequence of points 3 and 4

6. Kraft's accommodations
7. The constant vacuuming

Kraft himself would probably agree with this list, although he would certainly change the order of importance.

You know, he'd said on the evening of his arrival, to István, who now went by Ivan and whose American wife had already gone to bed, leaving the two men alone at the dining table with a Californian red wine and dense chocolate cake, you know, I need the money. More than any of the others. I need it to buy my freedom. I'll leave Heike, it won't break her heart, and I'll give them a shitload of money, all three of them, Heike and the girls. I'll buy my freedom, he said, and only the slightly forced ardor with which he described his plan would have alerted an attentive listener—which Ivan was not, nor had István ever been, Kraft had no need to worry—that this plan was not Kraft's idea.

f ine, Heike had said when she suddenly appeared in his office and tore him from the work he had taken up at a very late hour after having sat with one of the twins over a Latin translation while the other, following his repeated orders, sullenly manhandled the piano as Heike sat ensconced on the settee with her legs drawn in and her bandaged index finger held reproachfully aloft, staring fixedly at the television screen, on which a dwarf was cavorting between bearskins with two bare-breasted women. Fine, she'd said, go to Stanford and win the ridiculous competition, at least then we'll be able to put an end to this experiment.

Calling the last fourteen years an *experiment* struck him as unwarranted, so it took him a moment to realize that she was referring to their marriage and while he was deliberating whether he should express his hurt or rather, in light of this unexpected way out, ignore her remark, Heike was once again too quick for him and had already vanished from his office by the time he had decided on the first option, which he had calculated to be a stronger position for the negotiations that would inevitably follow. And so he'd had to follow her into the bathroom, where all his hopes crumbled since he found Heike ministering to her finger with a large bottle of antiseptic and demonstrating very clearly their injury deadlock.

Kraft had just reached this bathroom scene in his recollections when he caught sight of Newfoundland below him and the North American continent soon after. He recalled the undignified negotiations with reluctance. Four weeks, he had stipulated, he needed four weeks in Stanford to prepare the presentation. At least it was clear even to Heike that there wasn't the slightest chance he would win if he had to write his essay for the competition at home, squeezing it in between familial and professional duties, that he needed quiet and distance to answer the difficult question *What is the source of evil and what can be done about it?* He would have to marshal whatever shreds of optimism he had left to justify why whatever is, is right; and it was also clear to Heike that the farther away from her he was, the better he would do it. She conceded him two weeks, those were her terms, and not even his eloquent description of how elegantly a victory would solve the practical problems of their broken home—he surprised even himself by mentioning it—could persuade her to change them. This, my dear Kraft, she said, addressing him for the first time by their shared family name, is not the best of all possible worlds, and left the bathroom.

That night Kraft wrote a long e-mail to Ivan accepting the invitation to participate in the contest and asking if he might stay with him for two weeks before he lay down, back to back, next to his sleeping wife and, unable to fall asleep for a long time, gradually worked himself into a state of rage as the bells of the Collegiate Church tolled every quarter of an hour, a rage stoked by the regularity of Heike's breathing, which struck him as unsuitably serene, and by the sense of failure that came from his realization that the way out of the dead end into which he had maneuvered his life had not come through incisive critical reflection about the world—that was how he liked to describe his profession, which he also considered a way of life—but instead, as was now undeniably clear, from the world of finance, even if—and this seemed to add insult to injury—that liberating sum had first to be won through incisive critical reflection.

And because he had managed to keep a small ember of this rage glowing through the weeks and across the Atlantic, it was easy to re-kindle the fire during the interminable wait on arrival in Atlanta as a beagle in a chest harness from border control insisted on sniffing urgently and for the third time Kraft's backpack, which he had set down between his feet on the worn carpet. This gave the dog's ponytailed mistress grounds for a thorough inspection of his bag, an inspection from which she would not be dissuaded by Kraft's explanation in a remarkably nervous, even guilty tone that the dog was probably agitated by the smell of a mortadella sandwich that one of his daughters, he couldn't determine which because as usual they'd accused each other, had left in this very backpack—his own, he stressed—after she had borrowed it without permission for the May hike—here Kraft couldn't think of the English word, so he first tried *May perambulation*, then seeing the officer's uncomprehending look, followed with *spring . . . or let's say early summer stroll*, an expression that, as soon as he'd said it, sounded to him improper in connection with his daughter and left him worried that it somehow made him appear even more suspicious. The officer, however, seemed far less concerned with his daughter than with the health of her dog, who, tail wagging, had taken advantage of the brief conversation to bury his nose in Kraft's backpack before being pulled back by his mistress who asked Kraft in a surprisingly matter-of-fact tone without the slightest hint of disgust for information about the mortadella sandwich, whether it was still in the backpack, which Kraft indignantly denied, adding that he would hardly be traveling around in September with a sausage sandwich from the month of May; as was proper, he had disposed of it, or rather, what was left of it, but the smell had obviously penetrated the fabric of the backpack. For a moment he was tempted to describe the state of mummification in which he had found the snack after it had spent the entire summer in said backpack in the attic, which was often unbearably hot and arid, but since the dog and his mistress were losing interest in him, Kraft bit his tongue and turned his attention back to his rage, which had been further fanned by the vague sense of humiliation he experienced after every meeting with uniformed authorities and that was now burning freely. On the connecting flight, with the help of a scotch and a pack of wasabi peas, Kraft's rage mutated into a sense of inevitable victory that led him to greet Ivan in the arrivals hall of the San Francisco airport so extravagantly, as if he were hugging his trainer in the Roubaix velodrome, that the back-slapping seemed a bit excessive even to his friend Ivan, formerly known as István.

f or the rest, it wasn't easy for the two men to recover their former closeness, which had worn away to a meager remnant over years of encounters as irregular as they were haphazard, at conferences and congresses in far-flung towns between Bielefeld, Tampere, and Canberra, and the more they felt obligated by the loss of a sense of solidarity to celebrate and glorify their old intimacy the shabbier that remnant appeared to each of them individually, of course, since neither would ever mention it to the other.

Theirs had been a "thumbs up each other's ass" kind of intimacy as Schlüti, Richard's roommate at the time, characterized it at the top of his voice before slamming the door behind him on the first warm spring day in 1981 and storming down the still clammy stairwell of the house on Grunewaldstraße in Berlin's Steglitz district. Schlüti wasn't entirely wrong, even if his words did betray the bitterness of a roommate grown obsolete. Richard Kraft and István Pánczél did, in fact, demonstrate their attachment with an obtrusively staged physical proximity that would have at least theoretically allowed for such an unusual placement of thumbs, although it was the furthest thing from their minds; their love was of a purely political and ideological nature.

K raft, who was registered as studying economics, philosophy, and German literature but was also assiduously attending lectures in the history, sociology, and political science departments, enjoyed a reputation in the Free University of Berlin at the time as a brilliant thinker who, at twenty-three, had already read almost everything you had to read and as one of those students who was destined for an impressive academic career. However, because he was merely one of several such students, he looked for an effective way to distinguish himself from the others and to this end he turned to Thatcherism, an ideological current that was sure to isolate him sufficiently from the rest of the student body and make him the most unusual of the most promising students and thereby, in a mysterious way, make him come off as the most promising of the most promising.

Naturally, he was shocked on the morning of January 20, 1981, when a young man unknown to everyone in the auditorium took the floor during a lecture on Althusser, identified himself as a Hungarian dissident and political refugee, and in broken German began a loud and rather off-topic defense of Ronald Reagan, extolling his swearing-in as a historic moment and turning point in world history, a beacon in the fight against the communist oppressors and their subservient lackeys in the humanities faculties in the free world. At first Kraft was afraid this man would usurp his territory and with it his unique selling point, but he quickly realized that this István Pánczél with his hair pressed flat against the back of his head was, in fact, a marvelous ally who would lend Kraft's lonely struggle against the powerful state not only the legitimacy of injustice inflicted on his own body, but also the intellectual sheen of an Eastern European chess master. István was, after all, a member of the Hungarian delegation sent to West Berlin for the university chess championship, where he had taken advantage of the opportunity to defect.

At least, that was Pánczél's version of the story, which he eagerly recounted at every possible occasion, and which was by no means a fabrication; not, that is, if one took a rather flexible approach to the truth, since István withheld the fact that he owed his spot on the chess delegation to the ivory-colored polyester jerseys with which the Hungarian Chess Federation outfitted its players, because after two hours the shirts began to smell as if the wearers were not moving little wooden figures over a board, but were competing in a wrestling match. István, who had failed spectacularly in the qualifying tournament, was only brought along to Berlin because they needed someone to wash the players' sweaty shirts in the hotel sink at night.

When the noise of an Ikarus tour bus woke him before dawn on January 20, István looked out the hotel room window and saw his teammates, who had come in last place in the championship, boarding the bus with tired faces. By the time he ran down to the parking lot, still half-dressed and carrying a pile of freshly washed jerseys and a hastily packed suitcase, all he could do was watch the light blue bus thread its way through traffic toward Budapest. His absence was not noticed until the bus was outside Prague and so the trainer, the surveillance officer, and the players took turns blaming each other in a Czechoslovakian highway rest stop for forgetting to wake the shirt-washer Pánczél until they agreed on an adventurous tale of how the young man had defected using the most refined and subtle of ploys.

All the while, István sat on his bed in the West Berlin hotel room and waited in vain for the blue bus's return. In the dawning light, he cobbled together a story with astonishing similarities to the one his teammates had constructed at almost the same time, stuffed the ivory-colored jerseys into a large plastic bag, grabbed his small suitcase, and snuck out the hotel's rear exit. He wandered aimlessly for two hours through wintry Berlin sometimes feeling like a sock left behind under the bedspread, sometimes feeling his chest swell with the presentiment of a new freedom. He found refuge from the cold at last in an empty university auditorium and in the room's silence made the story he had just invented his own; and when the room began to fill and a lecturer who struck him as unbearably effusive began to speak of a French Marxist confined to a psychiatric asylum, István sealed the deal by screwing up his courage, interrupting the speaker, and presenting himself to the public for the first time as a Hungarian political refugee.

chapter two

We see precisely this most characteristic look just before the perpetrator enters the cross aisle! He keeps his head facing forward, only his eyes flit over the shopping carts. This [. . .] glance is so peculiar, it has so far never been observed in any honest customer.

—RICHARD THIESS

What particularly torments Kraft is that he cannot theoretically comprehend the wallpaper. He is convinced he should be able to make something of it. The same goes for all the furnishings, from the aforementioned eggshell-colored wallpaper on which robin redbreasts, beaks wide open, keep company with delicately drawn wild strawberries in an irritatingly regular pattern, to the sports trophies carefully aligned on the white rattan shelves, the modest narrow bed under the sloping ceiling of the attic room with its white enameled iron bed frame on which Kraft cools his overheated feet at night, and the similarly white lathe-turned child's desk across from a refurbished antique dresser. What is hidden behind it all is completely obvious: the idea of a happy childhood, an ideal family, and the firm conviction that the memory of this happiness can be preserved forever in this little girl's room. Just like the posters of enormous, sweat-drenched, long-retired basketball players that still adorn the walls of McKenzie's room, players she must have worshipped in the years before she left her parents' home for college in Poughkeepsie. Kraft had the sense that a happy childhood of this kind was a very American idea. It wouldn't make an impression on anyone in Europe, Kraft thinks, at least not in Germany and certainly not in Austria. Quite the opposite, in fact. Too carefree a childhood seems to him almost a guarantee for a future flippancy, which strikes him as frivolous and certainly not conducive to incisive critical reflection about the world.

He knows, however, that this theory is too vaguely formulated, not rigorously defensible. At least, he lacks reliable data. He is usually untroubled by such scruples when, finding himself yet again too far on the periphery in debates with his colleagues, he throws out an all-too-precipitous proposition he cannot support ad hoc with any data but that will nonetheless catapult him back to the center of the discussion. For that he can always rely on a theory jerry-rigged from his inexhaustible mental reserves. For compatibility, a common thread woven from late Heidegger, Nietzsche, or Schopenhauer, then for a border, some edging from Huntington's thick undercoat, for the weft, a few suitable stitches from an obscure, no doubt justly forgotten Chilean economist of the Chicago school he'd read in the early '80s and could still quote now, thirty years later, thanks to his phenomenal memory, along with a half-needle's length of Finkielkraut for indignation and a half-needle's length of Hölderlin for soul, for authenticity, a few loops from his essay, just published in *Merkur*, and as an ironic sealant, but also as a precautionary escape route, he drops in a few stitches of Karl Kraus. Kraft usually excelled at doing all of this off the cuff and engagingly enough to draw everyone's attention back to him, admittedly with a collective eye roll but rarely any substantial objections. Tonight, however: nothing. No matter how assiduously he clicks his needles, theory leaves him without a stitch. Was it the lack of an audience? But that's usually no problem since he can always conjure one up, imagine one into existence to suit his needs or mood, either a group nodding in agreement, with one or two pairs of eyes fixed on him, the speaker, wide with admiration and preferably blue, or the so-called pearls-before-swine scenario: a herd of individuals shaking their heads in disagreement, too trapped in their ideological obstinacy to even want to try to understand, thus spurring him to surpass himself. But not tonight.

Not tonight and not on the previous nights either, nights when, even before ten o'clock, he had crept with leaden limbs under the quilt hand-sewn by Ivan's wife and immediately drifted into a light sleep, plagued by abstract dreams that got tangled in loops and feedback, only to wake with a start each night punctually at half past midnight and then spend the remaining hours until dawn in the company of the basketball players and robin redbreasts stretching their beaks in mute longing toward the ever unattainable baskets and berries on the pitched ceiling an arm's length above his head.

The discrepancy between Kraft's nightly state of exquisite emotional tension and the heavy, pervasive exhaustion of his aging body is intolerable. Eyes open wide, he stares into the semidarkness as if hoping to discover something, but he simply can't theoretically comprehend the wallpaper. And tonight, his seventh night here, he's suddenly no longer sure if those really are robins, so he turns on the light on the night table and searches the bookshelves, between Van Allsburg's *The Polar Express* and Oates's *Big Mouth & Ugly Girl*, for the paperback edition of *All About Birds* he had noticed two nights earlier.

Book in hand, he sits on the edge of the bed, looks in the index for *robin*, finds the entry on page 62, holds the book up to the wallpaper for a more exact comparison, but still isn't sure so he turns on the glaring ceiling light; no, not a robin redbreast. Definitely not. How could he have been so mistaken? For seven long nights. He exhorts himself to be more alert. The carpet under his bare feet suddenly seems suspicious to him; he'd rather climb back into bed.

But now he wants to know. Kraft shoves a pillow behind his back, though the pressure of the cast-iron bed frame against his spine is still pleasant, and leafs systematically through the book. Purple finch, page 102. Again he compares the illustration in the book with one of the countless birds on the wall. Yes, without a doubt, purple finches. Satisfied, he replaces the book and turns off the light with the switch near the door.

On his way back into bed, the light-colored carpet again intrudes unpleasantly on his awareness, but now, in his more conciliatory mood, disgust does not get the upper hand. Instead, Kraft thinks of the plump, tender little-girl feet that must have trodden this path countless times. Thus at peace with himself, with theory, with the wallpaper and the carpeting, Kraft slips back under the colorful quilt and closes his eyes in the certainty that sleep will mercifully descend on him and, indeed, the heaviness creeps from his limbs and pools behind his eyelids before sloshing through his optic nerve and into his excited brain like oil on troubled waters.

He almost, almost falls asleep. But then: the little-girl feet. He sees them clearly and in minute detail and the clarity of the image rips his eyes open and brings everything back, the purple finches, the wild strawberries, the sports trophies, and the basketball players. Little-girl feet. What's with the little-girl feet? It makes him uncomfortable. He is far too well versed in cultural theory, aesthetics, literature, pornography, and psychoanalysis not to understand immediately that he is entering treacherous waters. But he'd never had the slightest interest in anything like this. He doesn't want to entertain the thought again, and yet, nevertheless, he focuses as long as he can on that very image, in reality so alien to him, because he wants even less to think about the topic he should actually be focusing on. It's perfectly clear to him that this, unfortunately, is not a matter of forbidden lust. This has nothing to do with McKenzie's innocent little-girl feet. Although Kraft does not doubt that McKenzie, whom he knows only from the framed photographs lining the stairway wall, has charming feet and has surely grown into a charming woman who performs her duties well in the Ann Arbor treasury. However, not even thinking of the taxman helps at the moment. It's obvious what the little-girl feet are referring to but he can't let himself think of the twins now because then he would have to think of Heike, too, and that is something he cannot afford to do, not after the past few nights, not in the state he's in.

Whatever you do, don't think of little-girl feet now.

Still, that was a good moment. With him, Kraft, and his daughters' four small feet. The twins were in the habit of soiling their diapers at the same time, so Kraft built an extra-wide changing table by hand, which, mind you, he was not allowed to use until Heike had summoned a carpenter to certify that the table's load capacity was sufficient. Kraft had hung a mirror over the table in which the twins could see each other, so they wouldn't need to keep turning to look at each other; they stayed nicely on their backs and communicated with their eyes open wide and their little arms outstretched above the straps.

Kraft will always remember that moment when he grabbed the four wriggling little feet and rubbed them one after the other with Nivea cream and made the twins giggle by tickling their fat tummies. *I am a good father after all* shot through his head and this thought took him so much by surprise that he repeated it several times in a childish voice, nodding vigorously and raising his eyebrows at his daughters, who beamed at him with their blue eyes and clumsily grabbed at his fingers.

Why did this thought surprise him so? Because until that moment Kraft had not once felt it was justified, which is not exactly a credit to him given that the man we're dealing with here is by no means a modest one and he had at that point already been a father for twenty years, although to be fair, we shouldn't count the six years during which he'd had no idea he even had a child.

In any case, that thought and the memory of it had evolved over time, for if that notion had always brought him a feeling of consolation in the twins' early years, it now brought only feelings of uncertainty and occasionally even—like right now, in McKenzie's room—a sense of failure. And that is why Kraft does not want, on any account or under any circumstances, to think of little-girl feet. Not now, not in this state, ideally never again.

At least one thing hasn't changed, Kraft thinks as he looks at the small birds he had night after night mistaken for robin redbreasts. The twins still like to get themselves in deep shit at the same time. Just three weeks ago, for example, a store detective had called from the H&M in the pedestrian zone and asked him to come pick up his two daughters. And after he had made his way, accompanied by the sales clerks' sympathetic looks, to a small back office, he found the two maddeningly relaxed girls explaining to a young man with heavily gelled hair that anyways they had nothing to worry about because they couldn't be charged until they turned fourteen, which wasn't for two months. It wasn't the shoplifting that worried him, or the two pairs of identical, purposely frayed hot pants the girls had clumsily shoved into their oversize fake leather handbags because they wanted to save the 9.90 euros, even if it rankled him that they had been dressing exactly alike for a year, the source of one of the biggest fights he'd ever had with Heike. He had even won that fight, since he believed they had to raise two independent people, not the Kessler twins, but Heike was too young to know who the Kessler twins were and countered that there's nothing in the world cuter than two identically dressed blond twin girls, an argument he parried by pointing out that the Kessler twins had never married, a fate Heike didn't want to be guilty of inflicting on her girls and so she dressed the two girls differently from the start, although Heike always made sure that the colors didn't clash, until their daughters decided a year ago, from one day to the next, always to wear matching outfits.

That wasn't what worried him as he ushered the girls out of the back room with a severe look and serious words after forcing them to apologize to the man with the hair gel, something they did reluctantly, rolling their kohl-lined eyes and telling him, Kraft, their father, that the young man was hardly the one they should apologize to since he was not the injured party, or maybe he thought this guy was the famous Mr. Hennes or rather Mr. Mauritz; on the contrary, in fact, this guy should be grateful that they let themselves be caught stealing because if there were no more shoplifters, he'd be out on the street without a job. No, what worried Kraft was the fact that they weren't the slightest bit contrite, not at all sheepish, but already negotiating, maneuvering strategically, and denying everything.

They haggled over the most minute attribution of guilt, introduced completely irrelevant sideshows, weighed every word on a jeweler's scale. These were all techniques, he was perfectly aware, they had learned from their parents, for this was the principle by which Kraft and Heike steered their marriage once their shared enthusiasm for their "family" project had waned, right about the time Heike went back to work and the rope they had been pulling together had unraveled into a tangle of pettiness, thwarted desires, pride, and priorities toward which each brought a personal tally of sacrifices and efforts made.

An almost complete absence of generosity, that's the root of the problem. But where can you find any, Kraft wonders, where can you turn if there's none left in your own heart? Maybe there's still some generosity slumbering deep inside him, Kraft hopes, just submerged, and all it needs is a small sign from Heike, a hint of generosity on her part, and he would be able to be generous in turn. But why wait for Heike? Doesn't it work both ways? No, not in this case. Heike, he was certain, would shamelessly exploit any sign of generosity and construe it as her victory and his defeat. They had been fighting this battle for a long time and whoever let their guard down first would lose.

Kraft squeezes the white enameled bars of the bed frame one by one between his toes, presses his feverish soles against the cool iron, and notes with a pall of disappointment how quickly the metal warms up and the sensory discrepancy between his organic warmth and the lifeless cold he craves disappears. His craving is so acute and the certainty of disappointment so great that tonight he abandons his search for fleeting happiness on the last six bars of the bed's footboard. Kraft throws off the quilt, swings his legs over the edge of the mattress, sits up, turns on the night table lamp, and fishes yesterday's socks out of the laundry bag. Anyway, sleep is out of the question. Besides, he has a job to do. The question about the origin and purpose of evil and why whatever is, is nonetheless right is waiting for an answer, no, for *his* answer. And the beauty of it all is that this answer will solve their family problem, something that has become increasingly urgent since, despite their mutual assurances, they are obviously incapable of leaving the girls out of it.

In his socks, boxers, and T-shirt, he sits on the lacquered chair at the small, white desk, pulls from his backpack his laptop and the thin pile of papers he has Ivan's secretary print out fresh for him every day even though he rarely adds anything new, and as he reads his notes, as useless as they are fragmentary since they do not marshal a shred of support for optimism, he feels his creative energy dissipate. Brooding gloomily, he sits in the light of the desk lamp. Maybe he should read Poser's technodicy essay again? Yes, that's the right approach. There, right on the first page, the problem of evil is presented in its simplest form, in the words of the Church Father Lactantius in his treatise *On the Anger of God*:

> Kraft either wants to eliminate evil and cannot, or he can but does not want to, or he neither can nor wants to, or he both can and wants to. If he wants to but cannot, then he is weak, which does not apply to Kraft; if he can but does not want to, then he is spiteful, which is equally foreign to Kraft's nature. If he neither wants to nor can, then he is both spiteful and weak and therefore not Kraft. But if he wants to and can, which is the only fitting thing for Kraft, where then does evil come from and why does he not eliminate it?

Yes, indeed, why does Kraft not eliminate it? Because he lacks optimism. He falls into gloomy brooding again. But as he sits there, all the heaviness seeps out of his body and is replaced by a clayey emptiness. He suddenly feels very light. Now, right now, he could fall asleep, if only he could sleep sitting up since on no account does he want to return to the finches and wild strawberries. So he remains seated and slips into a kind of trance in which four little pink feet slathered in skin cream dance before his eyelids. Kraft will get no closer to sleep tonight.

three

Lo now, his strength is in his loins, and his force
is in the navel of his belly. He moveth his tail
like a cedar.

—JOB 40:16-17

reakfast is a ceremony. A beloved tradition, a family
ritual, so why should we give it up just because our
daughter has moved out? Ivan asked on the first
morning. Ivan, Kraft has to admit, is always in a good mood
early in the morning and try as he might, he can't remember
this ever being the case with István. Ivan's wife, Barbara, sits at
the breakfast table in checked flannel pajamas, a suggestively

unattractive outfit that strikes Kraft as inappropriately private and that creates a sense of intimacy he finds hard to bear, so he concentrates on the rapidly lengthening bar on his tablet indicating its progress downloading the latest edition of the *Frankfurter Allgemeine Zeitung* and starts hectically tapping the link to the lead story with his middle finger, making the picture of the federal minister of finance jump out at him and shrink back in quick succession until he energetically swipes it to the left into his device's working memory, which creates the momentary illusion that the minister's wheelchair is rolling backward off the stage at the World Economic Forum. Ivan, meanwhile, drapes the bacon strips he dried out on a strip of parchment paper in the microwave over the fried eggs in an X and puts the plate in front of his wife, brightening her morning with sunnyside-ups as he does every day, upon which she assures him once again that he is an angel. Then he sits at the table satisfied, sips from his Mexican-stoneware mug, and remarks that now that they have Kraft with them at the breakfast table, things are a bit like they used to be. Kraft is reasonably certain that Ivan is not thinking of their days eating yogurt from the carton while standing in the kitchen on Grunewaldstraße; he smiles a rather strained smile and despite his best efforts can't prevent a quick glance at Barbara's feet, which she has propped on the edge of the chair, her knees bent. Ivan looks around him in delight and wipes a tear from the corner of his left eye, slipping his napkin under the steel frame of his eyeglasses in a practiced gesture.

This is no tear of emotion, just one of the innumerable tears that regularly drip from Ivan's bleary eye and have ever since June 11, 1982, when Ruth flailed István's face with a yellow gerbera daisy, shouting, "Peace without weapons!"

*a*nd yet, that day had begun so well. István and Kraft were among the handpicked happy few allowed to watch the landing of Air Force One on the Tempelhof airfield. They no doubt owed this distinction to the city fathers' wish not to give the dynamic American president, who seemed almost youthful despite his seventy years, the false impression that West Berlin was populated only by older ladies whose lives were shaped by the triad of seduction, punishment, and redemption: seduced by the fascist promise of purity, grandeur, and eternity, followed closely by the punishment inflicted through the brutality of the Red hordes, a punishment many of them suffered with their own bodies, and then the subsequent healing process through internal and external application of colorful products that the economic miracle rained down on them in the form of raisins and pantyhose in an inexhaustible stream that only the American spirit coupled with German diligence could guarantee, which was the reason why they were all too ready to pay homage to this diligent spirit by waving little star-spangled banners. Having a throng of seniors represent a city that occasionally seemed about to suffocate under the burden of its history would give the wrong picture: that much was clear to those in charge. And so they were desperately seeking students willing to cheer Ronald and Nancy Reagan; however, most students had neither the time nor the desire and were already busy digging up the paving stones on Nollendorfplatz. The authorities were, therefore, happy to grant István's request that he be allowed, as a direct beneficiary, so to speak, to express his gratitude in person to the leader of the free world.

The light blue airplane slowed to a stop, rolling stairs were drawn up to it, secret service agents in brown suits exited the plane, and this alone was already enough to elicit exclamations of enthusiasm from István. A photographer with a fussy hairdo followed the agents, military music played, flags fluttered in the warm wind, and then the representative of the tutelary power emerged onto the stairs at 9:47, his hand in Nancy's, and she in a white dress suit. Reagan waved briefly, descended the stairs, stepped on Berlin soil, and at the foot of the rolling stairs saluted the officers of the American forces, shook Mayor von Weizsäcker's hand, inspected the regiment of GIs standing at attention, and shook hands over the barrier with a few Berliners, among them the ecstatic shirt-washer Pánczél and the promising student Kraft, who made their way after this uplifting moment back through the crowd as ruthlessly as they had earlier pushed their way to the front row, treading on old ladies' feet and separating from their families small children who had been clinging to their mothers' hands. They ran to their bicycles and raced past the Kaiser Wilhelm Memorial Church to the Charlottenburg Palace to ensure they had the best seats there, as well.

Kraft was suffering. As he always did when he had to share something important to him with too many other people: twenty-five thousand Berliners listening to the president's speech and cheering in chorus. Even for a good cause, this was too much conformism for Kraft. Naturally it was an exhilarating feeling to be on the right side of history, but did it really have to be so crowded there? István, on the other hand, was completely euphoric. He sang "Börlin bleibt doch Börlin" with an American accent the whole way home and came up with the disastrous idea of paying a visit to the women demonstrating for peace on the Theodor-Heuss-Platz so he could straighten out their twisted view of the world with the authority of someone able to speak from direct experience.

It was nothing less than his duty, of this he was convinced, and Reagan's words had filled with him the courage of a lion. Thus equipped, he was ready to confront a horde of hysterical communist shrews, unprotected and wielding his fate and his intellectual superiority as his only weapons. You could say he was fortunate that the invention of social networks and the internet was nowhere near the horizon that day and as a result the two companions didn't have the vaguest idea of the dramatic events taking place on Nollendorfplatz. Otherwise, Kraft would never have been able to keep István from facing down a shower of paving stones armed only with his fate and intellectual superiority and he would have walked away with more than a damaged eye. On the other hand, they knew the location of the women's demonstration from the newspaper because it was the one demonstration the authorities had not, in their solicitude, categorically prohibited.

With fluttering quiff and large half-moons of sweat under his arms, István, ready for action, cycled down Ahornallee and shouted over his shoulder to the reluctant Kraft that he was planning on asking the women demonstrating if they had ever thought to wonder whether they would still be allowed, under the political regime they were so avidly supporting, to do what they were doing right now? A formulation with which Reagan would conclude, almost verbatim, his second Berlin speech almost five years later, causing István, in his London flat, to leap off the sofa in front of the television and call out to Kraft that he had always suspected it, but now he had proof that the Americans had bugged him, the Hungarian dissident refugee, during his Berlin years, and had apparently kept the very highest levels informed.

he hundred or so police officers on the Theodor-Heuss-Platz had no trouble keeping the demonstration of the "women in mourning" under control. They stood calmly in loose formation before the five hundred for the most part young women, waving banners they'd lovingly decorated with images of doves holding olive branches in their beaks, pictures that betrayed a fair amount of artistic talent, and chanting, "*Sonne statt Reagan!*"* It may even be that the police were a bit bored, especially since they'd just learned over the radio that their colleagues on the other side of the city were facing a completely different situation and surely would have more opportunity to demonstrate their courage and let their truncheons speak. Perhaps that's why they let István, who harangued them while pointing again and again at the big REAGAN button on his lapel and waving his little American flag, walk through the security cordon with Kraft in his wake all the way up to the waist-high barrier, where he stridently served the women a taste of his intellectual superiority. They, however, seemed unimpressed, so he dished out some choice insults instead as the police officers looked on, amused. Kraft, meanwhile, sized up the misguided women and, shaking his head, thought up a few observations on the role of women in society. István, his courage fanned by the presidential words, ventured within an arm's length of the pacifists and chose as the target for his insults the one woman whose political and moral misguidedness Kraft regretted the most, since her broad face, her hair tied up in a bun, and her ample bosom, well-defined under her violet T-shirt—a hideous piece of clothing he attributed to her political confusion—radiated a maternal, fecund air. Kraft was enchanted. Just as he was wondering if she might eventually show

---

* A play on *Regen*, the German word for rain: "Sun not rain/Reagan!"

herself receptive to his arguments and allow him to lead her back to the path of righteousness, István appeared to have gone a step too far with his politically inflected obscenities; at any rate, the woman in question blew her top and whipped István in the face with her yellow gerbera daisy, shouting, "Peace without weapons!"

Tears flowed and blood spurted. Unfortunately, István's vitreous humor also spurted, his eye perforated by the wire a prudent florist had used to reinforce the gerbera, spattering its contents over István's shirt and his little portrait of the laughing president. Kraft dragged István, bellowing like a stuck pig and spouting Hungarian curses, to an ambulance standing nearby as the police took advantage of the opportunity to club away at the front row of the women. Kraft held István's hand as two paramedics tried to stop more gel escaping from his eye with gauze bandages, then strapped the young man to a stretcher and roared off to the Steglitz clinic, blue lights flashing. Kraft watched the ambulance pull away and suddenly Ruth appeared beside him. She was devastated, on the brink of tears; what had she done? And Kraft seized the moment, stoked her feelings of guilt by recounting István's spectacular escape at great length and in vivid detail—an account that he himself didn't know was completely fabricated—and described the manifold forms of repression István must have suffered in his homeland, until the stricken Ruth believed she had just blinded the unofficial leader of the Hungarian intelligentsia. She gratefully accepted the scrap of paper with Kraft's telephone number so she could call him that evening and enquire about the courageous dissident's condition.

When Kraft was finally admitted to visit his friend that evening, he found István rather taciturn under a blue blanket, a thick bandage wrapped at a slant around his head. Kraft tried to cheer him up by telling him he looked exactly like Moshe Dayan in the photograph that showed the general waiting stoically hour after hour on the edge of the Lītānī River to be evacuated, but he'd forgotten that István had crossed the Israeli off his list of personal heroes last year for being politically unreliable. Kraft protested, but was thankful that the nurses soon sent him home because he didn't want to miss Ruth's call. And so he waited impatiently by the phone on the sofa that had served as István's bed for the first few years of their friendship until Schlüti gave up in aggravation, stormed down the staircase shouting crude insults, and moved out, abandoning his room to the refugee Hungarian chess master. Ruth did, in fact, call and was very relieved to hear that István's eye could be saved and asked if she could accompany Kraft to the hospital the following day in order to apologize in person.

Kraft waited for Ruth at the clinic entrance. She showed up with a bouquet of yellow gerbera daisies, proof of a quirky sense of humor, a trait to which Kraft was particularly susceptible. Everything about her entranced him. He looked favorably on the broad hips and generous bosom, which had struck him the day before and over which she now wore a much more acceptable black blouse. A visit today, he was sorry to have to tell her, would not be possible since István had just been taken into the OR for a new procedure. In Kraft's defense, this was true. Kraft was a bit alarmed on finding that Ruth seemed much more self-possessed than the day before, so he decided to inform her of his suspicion that his friend had an extremely difficult relationship with hospitals, or at least such was the conclusion he'd drawn from a nasty scar on István's groin, the result of a traumatic experience his friend only ever alluded to obscurely. Kraft, however, could not have known that István never mentioned it because he didn't like to explain that he'd suffered an inguinal hernia while trying to lift a kitchen cupboard and after the operation the scar became infected due to inadequate hygiene. As a result, István became monosyllabic whenever he was asked about the pink bulge a full handbreadth wide and muttered something about the horrors of socialism, by which he meant the squalid condition of the Budapest clinic, but in Kraft's mind called up vivid images of the secret police's dismal cellars. Kraft described those images so graphically that he soon had Ruth in a state similar to the one she'd been in the day before and so willing to accept his invitation to go out for ice cream.

What was it about Ruth that appealed so strongly to Kraft? Well, for one, her maternal side. Not that she treated Kraft maternally, not at all; that would have had the opposite effect. No, she was, to his mind, a maternal figure. She seemed to him to be perfectly cast for motherhood and because he believed the family was the indisputable foundation of bourgeois life as well as the soul of the state, he intended to do his part in building a stable nation as soon as possible, and furthermore, because he couldn't do this without the active participation of a woman, a mother, he was smitten with Ruth. One could object that it all perhaps had less to do with the bourgeois soul of the state and more with the difficult personality of Kraft's mother, but that would be unfair to the young Kraft, given that, at the time he was eyeing Ruth's breasts over his coffee ice cream, he not only didn't think much of the Viennese quack, he held the doctor's writings in outright contempt. In any case, his enthusiasm for Ruth turned to rapture when she admitted tentatively—because in her circles such an attitude was frowned upon—that she didn't approve of day-care centers, not that she was fundamentally opposed to them, of course, because childcare played an important role in the liberation of women, but for her personally, putting children in a stranger's care was out of the question; for her, motherhood was simply too appealing. Kraft endorsed her view with vehement nods and had he deigned to read Cohn-Bendit's great word bazaar of a memoir at the time instead of waiting for the scandalized press to run excerpts thirty years later, he certainly would have asserted that children in day-care centers were fundamentally at the mercy of unwashed lefties and their grabby hands fumbling at the little ones' flies, and with this assertion he would have spared a number of people some trouble. But, as it was, Ruth was spared this hard-hitting argument, one she presumably would have found unappetizing enough to turn her back on Kraft and her half-eaten banana split. Instead, she told him about studying to be a sculptor, which fanned Kraft's ardor even more as he found artistic people exciting and he immediately told himself that being a sculptor was a profession that could be easily cut back in the case of motherhood, both in the size and weight of the individual works and in terms of the time devoted to it. Kraft succumbed completely when Ruth told him her family name: she was a Lambsdorff. Kraft was over the moon despite her assurances that she was only very distantly related to the illustrious count and federal minister for economic affairs he idolized and that she had never met him personally, nor did she have the slightest desire to, unless it were to whack him in the eye with a gerbera daisy.

K raft was in love. And so it was that every third night he slipped out of the apartment on Grunewaldstraße under the pretext of devoting a few more hours to studying a work on double-entry bookkeeping by the Franciscan monk Luca Pacioli, a tome that was unfortunately only available for consultation in the reading room, and so left István behind on the sofa with a thick gauze bandage over his left eye and the *Knight Rider* videocassettes he owed to his acquaintance with a nurse of American descent. It was a betrayal, Kraft knew this, a double betrayal. Not only was he lying to his friend in such a difficult time and leaving him on his own, but, much worse, he was meeting with his friend's attacker, the woman completely and solely responsible for his sorry state—even if Kraft had in the meantime come to the conclusion that István shared some of the blame because of his provocations. But István would have none of it. He swore that as soon as he could see with both eyes again, he would search all Berlin for that socialist battle-ax—and he meant *all* Berlin, in case she'd defected to the East since the attack—and bring her to justice. Kraft didn't contradict him but excused himself again for his rendezvous with Pater Pacioli. The impossibility of balancing his moral debit and amorous credit almost tore him apart. He loved his valiant and clever comrade in arms István Pánczél, who had had to endure so many difficulties, but he also loved the very maternal future mother of his future children, his own personal Lambsdorff. It almost tore Kraft apart, but didn't prevent him from taking advantage of the opportunity, when István had to undergo another procedure, in which an ophthalmologist from the Federal Republic definitively ruined the shirt-washer Pánczél's left eye in a West Berlin hospital supported by American aid, presented by the sofa now freed up for two days to deluge Ruth with a stream of blather until she finally yielded to him and conceived their first child.

We know why Kraft was so smitten with Ruth, but we don't know what it was Ruth saw in him. Difficult to say. It wasn't his looks, even though Kraft was an attractive young man and attractive young men weren't exactly lining up to admire her broad behind. No, nor was it his compliments, even though she wasn't immune to them. Was she attracted by their differences? Differences that were most obvious in the political and ideological spheres? No, it wasn't their differences either; these only left her muttering a litany of what-on-earth-am-I-doings into her quilt. When all was said and done, Ruth had a soft spot. Not for Kraft, even if that's what it looked like. No, it wasn't at all a soft spot for anything in particular. It was a soft spot that is best described as, simply, a soft spot. A fundamental soft spot. An existential soft spot. A soft spot that occasionally overpowered her, floored her, hit her like a steamroller and left her powerless to resist anyone who came along to pick her up. She was well aware she had this weakness biding its time inside her, waiting only to seize its moment, but what she didn't yet know was that it had something to do with men and with a particular kind of man at that; she was susceptible to the biggest windbags around, and she succumbed to them without a word and in almost no time at all. She found their blathering so terribly exhausting that for her it was always too late from the start and she rarely escaped. But at the time she met Kraft, she did not yet understand the nature of her weakness. The scales only fell from her eyes on her fortieth birthday when she found herself trembling in front of Louise Bourgeois's *The Destruction of the Father* in Hamburg's Deichtorhallen, but by then she had read Freud. That, in fact, was one of the first things she did after divorcing Kraft.

As a result, she often yielded to windbags in those days, but it was rarely the case that those windbags, like Kraft, kept up a continuous stream of babbling, even in moments of passion, and left her so weak that for three weeks she didn't have the strength to leave her room, least of all to see Kraft, or even talk to him on the phone. Nor did she have the energy to open his daily letters. This left Kraft cut to the quick, his dreams of an ideal bourgeois family life fizzling like farts in the void, seated on the couch next to István, with whom he could not share his heartache for obvious reasons, letting himself be enticed by Michael Knight into shallower but much less painful realms.

One day Ruth was suddenly certain she was pregnant. She was certain but she took a pregnancy test just to make sure and then summoned Kraft to the Diener on Grolmanstraße to inform him of his paternity and take the subsequent unavoidable steps toward family life. Kraft, full of hope, arrived at the restaurant a quarter of an hour early and because he didn't know anyone in the Diener—it wasn't on his beat—he was forced to keep silent for a full fifteen minutes. An eternity, during which he prepared arguments to persuade Ruth of their shared future, such that Kraft's brain and heart brimmed like a reservoir about to overflow and the dam burst while Ruth was still taking off her raincoat, only to put it right back on, because for one brief, inexplicable moment her soft spot turned into a source of strength and as she looked down at the blathering Kraft the advantages of day care were suddenly crystal clear. She fled without a word into the summer rain. Kraft trotted home, and sat, his heart a gaping wound, next to his half-blind friend, whom he talked into watching the entire *Knight Rider* series again. He would not learn he was a father for six years.

four

Strength does not exist without kindness.

—HONORÉ DE BALZAC

raft likes to row. In a single. Having to match anyone else's cadence is not for him. And because he
so dearly misses his daily ritual of slicing silently
through the water of the Neckar River in the early morning
hours, the rapid, determined gliding, and the satisfaction of ad-
vancing solely under his own power, he begins to attribute the
cause of his intellectual crisis to its absence, and the half hour

spent on white lacquered machines set up in fixed rank and file in the Arrillaga Family Sports Center is, at best, a pitiful substitute and may even be exacerbating the crisis, so he borrows Ivan's old Ford Bronco and drives late in the afternoon to the university's boathouse, located on the shallow bay of the Redwood City port.

a student assigns him a sculling boat, and as they carry the slender, nearly weightless craft to the water, he conspicuously contracts his arm muscles and puffs up his broad chest under the tank top with the cardinal-red Stanford logo.

Kraft had bought the shirt that morning in the campus bookstore because the memory of the night before was throbbing so insistently in the back of his mind that no amount of the vacuum cleaner's howling and humming could drown it out until he came up with the idea of seeking deliverance in consumption, a strategy that occasionally worked because buying things requires at least a rudimentary level of optimism—indeed, why buy the most recent critical edition of Henry James's complete works in a linen slipcase if you're not assuming that life will go on, one way or another? Kraft hoped he could use that feeling as a foundation from which to struggle upward, step by laborious step, until he reached a level where pondering why whatever is, is right did not seem utterly ridiculous. But when he broke into a sweat while waiting in line for the cash register with the thirty volumes—in six shrink-wrapped linen slipcases—despite the frigid air streaming down from the air-conditioning vents, it was the purchase itself that suddenly seemed ridiculous. Ridiculous and witless. He would have to pay at least eighty dollars for excess baggage weight, not to mention the fact that he would also need a new suitcase for the books and, besides, the mere thought of having to read thirty volumes of Henry James made new beads of sweat pearl on his forehead.

He reluctantly put the books back, fully aware that his failure with this purchase had irrevocably ruined the day. He therefore used the opportunity to find a present for the twins in the Stanford merchandise section. As he made his way between the stands with key rings, the shelves of coffee mugs, the cardinal-red shower curtains, and miles of sportswear, he grew more uncertain with each step of what he could give his girls to make them happy, especially since he had no idea what size T-shirt or hoodie they wore, and with every piece of clothing he held tentatively in the air, the contours of his daughters' bodies in his mind's eye changed shape so that he no longer had any idea whether they came up to his chest or just to his waist or whether their slender shoulders were wider or narrower than a clothes hanger. At some point he grabbed a cardinal-red baseball cap and a nylon backpack embroidered with the university logo—a backpack would be useful, that much he knew—and headed back to the cashier with a tank top for himself as well. The student in front of him in line was wearing the outfit that was practically the school uniform and somehow got under Kraft's skin. Sneakers, T-shirt, and athletic shorts—particularly short shorts, he could not help noticing. The young woman's shorts were made of gray jersey emblazoned with the university's logo in large red letters and barely covered her rear end. Not that Kraft found this outfit especially tantalizing, nor did he find it at all outrageous—he was happy to leave outrage over barely dressed students to others. But somehow this getup seemed inappropriate because this hypertrophied sportiness was not compatible with intellectual labor, even if in this country there seemed to be a closer connection between training the body and training the mind than in Germany; he had, in fact, witnessed

Ivan promise the students in his seminar that by the end of the semester they could be confident they would be *well trained in late Heidegger*, an adjective that Kraft did not associate with the thinker from Todtnauberg, but instead with javelin throwing and jumping hurdles. What caught his attention were not her shorts first and foremost, but her spindly legs, limbs that looked like they had grown too long and too fast, protruding from her shorts like the legs of a deer— like his girls' legs. Kraft turned away, pushed his way out of line with murmured apologies, hung the cap and backpack on the closest rack, and went off to find the cotton shorts. He headed back toward the cashier with a light blue and a gray pair, but turned around halfway there and exchanged the gray ones for a second, identical light blue pair. This purchase satisfied Kraft far more deeply than a complete edition of Henry James ever could.

Having thus recovered his motivation, Kraft sat back down to work in the Hoover Tower. He wrote a witty paragraph on the Stendhal quote that God's only excuse is that He does not exist, then segued elegantly to several thoughts on the autonomy and self-determination of man, who was naturally and necessarily at the center of a modern theodicy. And yet he stumbled at the idea that in Silicon Valley even the evil of failure had been turned into a virtue by being presented as an opportunity. He had no idea how he could sell this idea as grounds for optimism. He watched his creative energy dissipate rapidly and so packed up his things, borrowed Ivan's SUV, and searched the unfathomable hodgepodge of single-story functional buildings that housed biotech and software firms, shopping centers, industrial facilities, and run-down single-family homes for the university boathouse. He parked in the boathouse lot and as he locked the car, he abruptly ducked his head, startled by a small aircraft from the nearby San Carlos airport that buzzed him like a lazy stag beetle.

Kraft eyes the bay, at least as much of it as is visible. A narrow, brackish canal, and behind it lies Bair Island, a reddish-brown stretch of marshland, as flat as a pancake threaded by countless meandering canals and punctuated by the masts of high-voltage electric lines. This isn't the Neckar, to be sure, but from Kraft's point of view there's nothing he can or would even deign to see that could justify the procedure to which he is now expected to submit: despite all the flexing with which he tried to display his fitness to row, the student categorically refused to provide him with oars. No, only Herb was authorized to give them out and even then only after detailed instructions on navigating the island's tides.

Herb has a white goatee and a pair of those sunglasses with lenses as iridescent as insect eyes that can make even a skinny retired physicist like this one look like someone capable of the dirtiest tricks. Kraft is on the defensive from the first *Hey, buddy* and tries his best to follow the downright complicated lecture on ebb and flow tides, current conditions, flow restrictors and channels, but when Kraft is on the defensive he's never at his best and tends to lower his guard and as a result Heike and the twins and somehow Ruth and her yellow gerbera as well overpower his consciousness and with it Herb's lecture, which is now covering something called the Corkscrew Slough and also the Steinberger Slough, along with the issue of turning either right or left, such turns being not only completely inadvisable in current tidal conditions but, more than that, dangerous to life and limb, and therefore to be avoided at all costs. Kraft nods eagerly, yes, he understands, it's strictly forbidden to get closer than so many feet to the seals and besides the whole island is a nature preserve and it's forbidden to set foot on it outside of a few marked paths. Fifty minutes, Herb impresses on him, that's all he's got to row the circuit, after that things get dangerous and a few places will become impassable. Herb finally lets go of the oars and forces on Kraft a waterproof bag for his cell phone, without which he won't let Kraft leave under any circumstances. Kraft climbs into his boat and because the vision of his four women during Herb's lecture has upset his equilibrium, the boat tips threateningly, and Kraft is certain that Herb is looking at him skeptically behind his insect lenses.

But after just a few strokes in which he can feel his muscles revive under his new shirt, the boat begins to glide and Kraft recovers his long-yearned-for calm. He has to admit that he had underestimated the place. After several hundred meters he leaves the port behind, glides in an elegant curve through the concrete flow restrictor and into Corkscrew Slough, and suddenly finds himself in the very middle of the avian world of Northern California. The herons nesting on the flat grasslands ogle him, necks elongated. Ducks of all colors paddle leisurely behind him. A raptor perches on a wooden post. Kraft stops, lays the oars flat on the water, and reaches behind him for the waterproof bag with his cell phone so that he can photograph this ornithological diversity and later identify the creatures with the assistance of McKenzie's *All About Birds*. Not that he's ever been very interested in birds, but his error with the robin redbreast has left him shaken and at least he will now be able to put the sleepless hours ahead, about which he is already apprehensive, to intelligent use. Kraft lets himself drift as he tries to zoom in to the feathered heads with his display by spreading his thumb and index finger on the screen the way the twins taught him, as if he wanted to pry the telephone's eyelids open to look for a stray lash. For this reason, and because he can't get the desired magnification, he leans far overboard, making the slender boat wobble alarmingly. Kraft has to grab for the oars to keep from capsizing. Let any who would reproach Kraft for his clumsiness first prove his own ability to grab two oars in a matter of milliseconds without losing hold of his cell phone, and all without being obliged, like our Kraft, once his balance was recovered, to associate the light splash he'd just heard with the painful knowledge that he had not, in fact, executed this tour de force. Kraft waits until his heart, which skipped several beats with the double fright, is beating regularly again, swears, reproaches himself, calls himself an idiot, smacks himself three times on the forehead for good measure, gives up the telephone for lost, and, after giving a duck circling his boat a venomous look, begins rowing again in order to get away from the site of his lonely humiliation as quickly as possible.

Corkscrew Slough is a credit to its name and winds in tighter and tighter turns through the marshes as if it wanted to make it clear to Kraft time and time again that it most certainly is not the Neckar River. Indeed, he toils mightily through the twists and turns and because he constantly has to look behind him, his neck is soon stiff. There can be no talk of contemplative gliding. He pulls with all his strength on the left oar only to have to even himself out by pulling hard on the right. The initially elegant curves give way to a frenzied zigzagging and before long the sculling boat runs aground with a grating sound. Kraft rocks his hips and, artfully applying the oars, manages to free the boat from the soft mud. As he does this, he notices how low the boat is sitting; he can now barely see over the surface of the land. Only the very tops of the highest buildings are visible, along with the mountain ridge behind them, over which a fogbank is rolling into Silicon Valley as it does every evening. The water level must have already fallen considerably. Fifty minutes, Herb had said, but how the hell was he supposed to know how long he'd been out already without his watch, which he'd left in a locker, or his phone, which he now misses twice as keenly in view of the seals that have suddenly appeared, stretched out in glorious nonchalance on the still damp mud- and sandbanks, goggling curiously at Kraft as he rows past. Now that's a photo opportunity that would have impressed the girls. There, less than eight meters away from him, is a huge pile of them, heaped together like sausages on a grill. Eight meters, Kraft calculates, is that more or less than twenty-five feet, and did Herb actually say twenty-five and not thirty-five? Then again, maybe the animals really are closer to twelve meters away from him, the number eight having perhaps simply been inspired by the story he's planning on telling the twins? Kraft gets tangled up converting yards and feet into the metric system with its thicket of shifting decimal points and is defeated by this anachronism of the Anglo-Saxon world. Better safe than sorry, he thinks, and tries to put as much distance between him and the fat bodies as the channel allows.

This, however, is easier said than done, because the channel is growing ever narrower due to the dropping water level, and mudbanks rise from the shallow water on all sides, requiring Kraft more than once to row a tortuous course that brings him far too close to the seals, something he absolutely wants to avoid after seeing one of these hefty creatures crawl out of the water and advance on dry land with astonishing agility by contracting and expanding its body in countless folds like the bellows of an accordion and then scale his dozing congeners, causing an outbreak of loud braying and an explosion of violence in the hitherto peaceful heap. Barks, howls, and yowls resound and Kraft takes note of the teeth bristling in their gaping mouths as chests smack against each other. The biggest one, a male, Kraft has no doubt, evidently feels especially disturbed by the impertinent newcomer and, rearing his massive body up, lets out a menacing roar that does not fail to have its full effect on either Kraft or the unwelcome seal. Kraft redoubles his efforts.

Fifty minutes: Herb's insistent words echo in his head. Fifty minutes are long past, Kraft knows this, but whether he's been out one hour or two, he cannot say. In any case, the fogbank has dropped low into the valley and in the office buildings the software developers and the marketing experts have turned on their ceiling lamps, which now glow dully through the haze. Kraft fervently hopes the fog will stop before the bay, but soon he can only make out the seals when he is close enough to smell them and they, startled by his sudden appearance, break out in agitated barking. At least, Kraft has the impression, the channel has grown deeper and less winding. It even seems to have straightened out and at the very moment he notices a faint roaring and gurgling, he feels the current grab the hull and pull it faster and faster forward. Kraft tries to fight it by digging his oars into the water, but the boat starts to rock violently, and he immediately realizes that all resistance is futile. He looks behind him and peers strenuously into the fog. The water around his boat revels in small swirls and dancing waves, and suddenly a wall looms out of the fog with a wide gap in its middle through which the water shoots in foamy agitation. Kraft lets go of the oars and grips the sides of his boat as it hops and dances and lurches. Still, he bravely keeps the narrow boat balanced; then, just as he passes the flow restrictor, one of the oars hits the wall, the boat turns sideways, Kraft throws his body from one side to the other, in vain: the boat capsizes. He has the presence of mind to pull the cord between his feet to free them from the shoes fixed to the boat's footrest and he falls into the water. He gashes open his knee on a submerged stone, the boat slams him in the back of the neck when he comes up for air, again the cold water closes over his head, the current grabs him, twirls him head over heels like a spin cycle, and pulls his gym shorts down his legs before he touches ground that is at least firm enough to push off from and he surfaces dazed, snorting, spitting, and making frenzied swimming motions. He makes it out of the current, leaves the boat for lost, his gym shorts too, and with powerful strokes he tries to reach dry land through the fog.

Before long he feels ground under his feet, but it offers no support. His bare toes sink deep into the slime and the seagrass wraps around his member and tickles his scrotum. He stretches out flat in the water and snuffles in the twilight. He certainly doesn't want to land in the middle of a pack of seals by mistake. Or maybe precisely what he should do is to crawl out of the water on his belly and howl pitifully, like the fluffy baby seals with their big, trusting eyes just before the club smashes in their heads—as he saw in the YouTube video the twins played for him, their eyes brimming with tears—and take advantage of the others' blubber to warm himself by slipping between their bodies. As the streetwise manager of his own catastrophes, Kraft knows the cold will soon be his biggest problem. He manages to grab a handful of grass and pull himself up. He hoists himself onto firm ground, gasping and smeared with mud. On his hands and knees, he peers into the fog. No, no seals nearby. No one to warm him, but also no one against whom, chest to chest, he will have to measure himself.

Kraft straightens up and peels off his ice-cold, soggy Stanford shirt. He stands naked in the marsh. He puffs out his chest and draws back his shoulders: Did he not just give death the slip? Did he not just elude danger on the strength of his own resourcefulness? Is that not ground enough to stand upright and to his full height? Kraft knows that he would normally dismiss this kind of virile and vulgar physical self-confidence with a disdainful smile, but at the moment it is of vital importance. Nonetheless, at the first gust of wind that sweeps over his broad chest, he feels his nipples contract and with them, his self-confidence. Shivering, he wraps his arms around his cowering body and focuses solely on the burning pain in his bleeding knee. He will die here, a miserable death from exposure, no, worse, Herb will rescue him, naked as he is, coated with mud, bleeding, helpless . . . Herb, that emaciated insect, that physicist with his tide models, his flow velocities, distances to maintain, and time windows; for him all these were nothing but variables in an equation from which all superfluity had been subtracted. What does a guy like Herb know about an individual's entanglements with the world, about the necessity for chance, about the beauty of the superfluous, about suffering, about humiliation? For a guy like Herb it can all be tallied, every evil offset by a good. Who the victim is plays no role, the important thing is for the equation to balance in the end. They call it elegance, those number jugglers. What does a guy like Herb know about elegance? The abstract splendor of the whole, perhaps. But what about his, Kraft's, concrete pain? His nakedness, his bleeding knee? The ferocity of the seals? The beauty of the herons? No, it's out of the question to let this Herb, this apostle of the system, rescue him. Not that physicist. Kraft must save himself. He has to get out of the marsh on his own and swim across the canal to the dock. Maybe, if he's lucky, he'll be able to get to his locker in the boathouse without being seen, that way he wouldn't have to face Herb without any pants; without a boat, it's true, but at least not naked. And he would have rescued himself.

Behind him, Kraft can hear the rushing and gurgling of the flow restrictor. He peers intently into the darkness. A cool breeze makes him shiver again but also parts the fog for a moment and clears a view of the cylindrical towers of the Oracle campus, their lights pulsating in the dusk like giant accumulators. That's good, now he knows roughly where he is. He has to keep heading slightly to the left until he reaches the large canal and from there he can look for the lights of the boathouse. Hesitantly, he puts one foot in front of the other; he, who never goes barefoot, is paying for it now as the stiff, salt-tolerant grass stabs his tender soles. If only he could see better where to put his feet, but now it's almost completely dark and the thick fog has closed in again. He stubs his toes on rocks, sticks, and poles. He inadvertently steps into a deep hole, twists his ankle, and screams with pain. If he's torn a ligament, it's all over for him. Then he will have to face death or Herb. He gingerly puts his weight on his sore ankle and takes a few tentative steps. Yes, he can do it. He is making progress, hobbling and limping, but progress all the same. Indeed, he advances slowly because the terrain is strewn with holes and pools and every few meters streams meander through the grass. The salt burns his wounds and the wind blows over his wet skin, making him shiver to his very marrow. With one hand he protects his wizened privates.

Would she be able to read about his death in the papers? Or about his humiliating rescue? The latter seems by far the most shameful, because with a touch of goodwill you could see the former in a somewhat tragically heroic light. Would the *San Francisco Chronicle* print a picture? NAKED GERMAN SCHOLAR RESCUED FROM BAIR ISLAND! Would this be the first thing she, Johanna, saw at breakfast tomorrow, thirty years after he made her so furious that she disappeared to California forever?

He has to admit, he makes better progress in the mud and the muck when he gropes his way forward on all fours, abandoning the upright gait he defends so ardently when he lectures his students. He abandons all thought as well, and surrenders himself completely to the subsoil, to the damp earth that squirts between his fingers, to the hard grass that gives him purchase, that he can grab, to the low bushes he has to avoid because they tear at his ribs, and occasionally to a stone, on which he can feel a last hint of warmth. When he lies flat on the ground, he can escape the wind. Now and then he raises his head and tries to orient himself. All at once the fog seems less impenetrable.

Kraft even believes he can make out a few lights. Maybe he's already very close to the canal, maybe, yes, he's definitely made it, and hope sprouts anew in his heart. Then the fog suddenly clears, blown away like a thin curtain of silk and lace, revealing the entire expanse of the valley. An endless twinkling and sparkling sea of light, the orange network of sodium-vapor lamps, the flashing lights on the landing strip, the yellow rectangles of thousands of windows, the shining and fading car headlights, a glow that illuminates the sky and bathes the marsh in a gentle light and, as if the fog had lain like cotton in his ears, he can now hear the sounds emitted by this beehive, a humming and buzzing of a thousand motors and myriad air-conditioning units, the thrum of work creating the digital future. Kraft rises again to his full height. Naked but on his feet, he stands in the wind. There, less than three hundred meters away, the center of the world stretches out before him, the engine of progress, the incubator of the future, shimmering, glowing, gleaming, it takes his breath away, floors him. Johanna, Johanna . . . how did I make you so angry? Kraft collapses, falls to his knees, covers his face with his hands in a gesture filled with a pathos that doesn't suit him at all, as if he had to shield himself from this concentrated charge of civilization that contrasts so drastically with his pitiful condition. In this self-imposed obscurity, this cave built from his own palms that smell of slime, grass, fish, and the sea, he surrenders to a crushing sense of guilt. An entirely unspecific sense of guilt. Still, he gets lost in it as in a dark, ancient city and it feels as if, behind the walls, hidden from sight, terrible things are happening and he isn't sure if he's guilty of all this evil or only guilty of not preventing it. But no one will be able to accuse him later of not trying to do anything. He musters all his strength of spirit and shakes the doors of this ancient city, but they don't give an inch and he remains outside, condemned to inaction, and all the while, as if from a great distance, a call echoes through the empty streets: *Richard, Richard*—with a Californian accent.

Kraft abandons his dark city and his moldy cave and, ignoring the pain, he rises and totters toward the call. He finally also notices the sound of an outboard motor and sees a beam of light sweeping over the marsh. There, in the canal, Herb stands at the wheel of an inflatable dinghy shouting Kraft's name at the top of his voice. *Here, here,* Kraft shouts, and sees Herb heave to and run the boat's rubber bow aground. Kraft covers the last few meters and feels the cone of light catch him. He freezes like an animal surprised by a flashlight and drops his arms. Herb leaps out of the boat and approaches him. *You've lost your pants, buddy,* he says, and spreads a blanket over his shoulders. Kraft weeps.

five

In all the different countries fate has had me travel through, and in the taverns where I have been a servant, I have met a vast number of people who loathed their existences; but I have only met a dozen who have voluntarily put an end to their misery: three black men, four Englishmen, four Genevans, and a German professor named Robeck.

—VOLTAIRE

t he shame doesn't come till later, along with his astonishment that he broke down so quickly and so completely and let himself fall on all fours. It only hits him the morning after, when he sits down very early at his desk in the Hoover Tower reading room, surprisingly well rested— for the first time since his arrival in California he doesn't feel tired—and is confronted anew by the former secretary of defense's scornful look.

erb had returned him to the dock without a word and once Kraft had reassured him that he really didn't require any medical treatment, he let Kraft take a long hot shower. Afterward, they sat facing each other in the boathouse's common room for a long time. Herb made cocoa and Kraft drank it despite his dislike of milk. Good old Herb, whose white beard, in the light of recent events, now struck Kraft as reassuring and benevolent. Kraft was grateful to Herb for keeping silent and not delivering any lectures, something he could not have borne. But after a while it was Kraft who could no longer stand the silence. He broke into nervous laughter and launched into a half-hearted self-justification, but broke off in the middle of the first sentence. Herb sipped his cocoa and said, *Shit happens.* They sat in silence a while longer until Herb cleared his throat, set down his cup with an *anyway*, and informed Kraft that unfortunately he would have to charge Kraft for the boat and the oars, an amount slightly higher than Kraft's monthly income. This wrung another bout of nervous laughter from Kraft and he tried to relativize it in turn with his own, *Shit happens.*

hen he got back to the house, Ivan and Barbara were at a university soiree. Kraft lay down on McKenzie's bed, leafed through a few pages of *All About Birds*, fancied he recognized a few of the birds he had seen, especially the duck that, it had seemed to him, had laughed at him when he dropped his phone, but exhaustion soon overcame him and with it, mercifully, a deep, dreamless sleep.

At breakfast, the unfamiliar feeling of being well rested allowed him to depict the experiences of the day before as an adventure, with him playing the lead, and his self-confidence was restored to such an extent that he did not omit the detail of the lost shorts. He conjured up the image of a naked warrior, standing tall, his chest out, wrestling with pitiless nature, a depiction that brought a blush to Barbara's cheeks over her flannel pajamas, a blush Kraft completely misinterpreted, and swelling with a small, foolish sense of pride, he put more fuel on his story's fire.

his restored equilibrium, however, proves fragile and no match for Rumsfeld's cold eyes, which seem to be searching deep inside Kraft for the diffuse sense of guilt that infused him in the marsh at the thought of Johanna. And because this threatens to undermine his foundations once again, Kraft taps, so to speak, his opponent's aggressive energy by reaching for the former secretary of defense's shameless rhetoric, and he tries to dismiss his rattling at the doors of the City of Guilt the night before as an encounter with an unknown unknown, a categorization that strikes him at the moment as particularly judicious, given that until he'd experienced that sense of guilt, he hadn't known that there was such an emotion in him, not to mention the fact that he had no idea what he should be feeling guilty about, but here Kraft's erudition once again gets in his way. He's familiar with the objections raised by Žižek—a thinker he profoundly disdains for clinging to Marxism and whom he envies just as deeply for his brazen indulgence, even celebration of his own tics as well as for his marriage to an underwear model trained in Lacanian psychoanalysis. In Žižek's view, the mention of the unknown unknown usually indicates a denial of the unknown known, that is, of the Freudian unconscious, or as Lacan called it, "knowledge that does not know itself." Thus did Kraft's own knowledge catch him out and leave him no choice but to drop that painful subject and turn to an even more painful one that he had so far successfully suppressed— the financial damage he had inflicted on himself with his careless and, yes, idiotic actions.

Have we not already presented Kraft's financial situation as one of the reasons for his writer's block? Made clear the existential necessity of impressing the prize jury as a result of his familial and financial circumstances? Is it not perfectly understandable that he would be paralyzed with shame at the thought of returning to Heike, not simply empty-handed, but with a debt for the sunken carbon-fiber boat amounting to a month's salary, and that this paralysis is hardly propitious for his efforts to formulate an argument proving that whatever is, is right?

Go, win, come back with the prize money so we can all have our freedom again, Kraft can hear Heike saying, and can't help but think of her bunion.

Considering the immensity of the task, we must, indeed, have compassion for Kraft. Many before him have buckled under such pressure.

Kraft can no longer withstand the former secretary of defense's gaze. He lowers his eyes in defeat, closes his laptop, and shuffles out of the reading room. In the lobby of the Hoover Institution on War, Revolution, and Peace he meets two nervous security guards in red jackets listening raptly to voices coming from their two-way radios. They only notice him when he begins rattling the locked door. *Sir*, they call, *Sir*, and it takes him a moment to realize they're talking to him: *Sir, you can't leave now. We must ask you to stay inside.* Had he not seen the crime alert sent to all members of the Stanford community by text as well as by e-mail? No, Kraft had not, and because he doesn't like to be locked in and fundamentally dislikes being told what he has to do or cannot do, he answers rudely that his phone is unfortunately lying on the bottom of the San Francisco Bay and it's very possible that an impertinent crested grebe has read the crime alert in his stead and is now in a state of panic, and besides, on principle, he only checks his e-mail after lunch. *Sir,* one of the guards says, *you have to keep your phone with you at all times. For safety reasons,* the other one adds. Kraft says that he is precisely on his way to replace his phone, something that will be hard to do if he can't leave the building. Unfortunately, that's not possible at this time, he is told, a gunman has been spotted on campus and Kraft is asked to remain in the building and away from any windows until the police have clarified the situation. Kraft notices that the key is in the door's lock and as the two men in red windbreakers turn their attentions back to their crackling radios, he seizes the moment, reaches the door in three long strides, turns the key in the lock, yanks the door open, and flees, all to the security guards' frantic cries. On the stairs, he looks over his shoulder but sees only one of the guards peering fearfully through the gap of the door before closing it quickly.

Emboldened by this act of self-determination, Kraft crosses the deserted campus with measured steps. Why not? Being shot down by a madman on one of America's elite university campuses hardly seems like one of the worst conclusions to his biography and as he thinks of how difficult this would make it for his colleagues to defend optimism at the conference and to defend the claim that whatever is, is right just days after one of their own has been murdered in cold blood, he feels a thrill, steps out of the building's shadow, and ambles across the broad oval lawn in front of the main entrance, offering an ideal target to any gunman.

Kraft is all alone. The students on their bicycles are gone, the young men lounging on the grass, baring their chests to the sun, have vanished. The circle of dreadlocked hacky-sack players has disbanded and taken refuge indoors. Fled, too, are the families posing proudly with their freshman students in front of the university logo of red and white flowers. In the distance a campus security SUV drives slowly past. Kraft stops in the middle of the green lawn and spins around once. A shiver runs down his spine; a faint emotion washes over him; nothing happens. He continues on, crosses the parking lot on the edge of the oval, lingers in the shadow of the tall eucalyptus trees, and breathes in their cough-drop scent. The Rodin figures sit, abandoned, on their pedestals in the Cantor Arts Center sculpture garden. Kraft stops in front of *The Gates of Hell* and under the brooding gaze of *The Thinker* he tries to lose himself in looking at the figures, but he can't get free of himself, can't find the necessary remove from his own present required for the contemplation of such a masterpiece and that is why he also can't leave behind his store of knowledge, which collapses over him like an old card catalog and buries him under a mountain of index cards: the fall of the angels, Dante, Baudelaire, *Les fleurs du mal*, and his brain starts buzzing, *I have but one hope / It is that my Death, hovering like a new-formed sun / will coax the flowers of my brain to bloom*, and *It is Death that consoles, alas! and that makes me live; / My life's only goal, my only hope*, and while he's at it, he yields completely to the temptation to fraternize with Baudelaire and release *The Thinker* from his pose. *The world will end*, Kraft declaims. And because this fellow Kraft considers an obvious kindred spirit does not raise his bronze head from his fist, he adds: What's the problem? Has the California sun, beating down on your head day in, day out, dried up your brain? That can't be healthy for a Frenchman. *The mechanical,* he continues, again seeking refuge in Baudelaire, though not quite to the point—still, it's important to him to unburden himself of the thought at this moment—*will have Americanized us to such an extent and progress will have so atrophied in us all that is spiritual, that nothing in the Utopians' dreams, however blood-soaked, sacrilegious, or unnatural, can be compared to the positive results.* The bronze statue, as is hardly surprising, remains silent and still, doesn't even flinch when a shot rings out very nearby. Kraft, however, is terrified. In anticipation of the bullet drilling between his shoulder blades, ripping his chest open, spattering his flesh over the Rodin and spraying his blood into the Inferno, he squeezes his eyes shut; nothing happens.

He walks along the deserted Quarry Road toward the shopping center and feels like a deer in the crosshairs, but since this image doesn't appeal to him, he corrects himself and tries to imagine he's a stag as tall as a man with fuzzy shreds of velvet hanging from his antlers. He even believes he can feel the weight of his mighty twelve-point rack; a heavy load, as he can tell from his straining neck muscles. Admittedly, this strain, like the burning sensation in his knee, is a vestige of yesterday's adventure, and because these pains remind him of his humiliation, his inexplicable collapse, his helplessness, and the eight thousand dollars for the boat, which in turn makes him think of Heike, waiting at home for the prize money, he longs again for the bullet to his heart and listens for the liberating shot. Then again, he reasons, if all goes well, he won't even hear the shot. Kraft doesn't understand the first thing about ballistics, but he is certain the bullet will travel faster than sound and hopes that he'll be dead before the latter reaches him. Mulling such considerations, he reaches the shopping center and is rather disappointed to note the buzz of activity there. Either the alert doesn't apply to this area or an all clear has already been issued. In any case, he has to admit that bleeding to death between a Victoria's Secret store and a Dunkin' Donuts would not be a particularly dignified end to his biography, or at least a much less suitable one than dying on a university campus.

Kraft enters the Apple store, a glass hall with a suspended roof of very thin steel and two long rows of refectory tables. The dully gleaming devices are spread out on the tables, screens smeared with greasy traces of innumerable fingers. Kraft looks for the table with the iPhones and leans over the devices, his hands behind his back. He doesn't want to touch them after having read an article in the *Deutsche Bahn* magazine that vividly described the microbiological life on touchscreens. Diarrhea instead of a gunshot to the head: not an option. A young man in a royal blue T-shirt bearing the image of an apple with a bite taken out of it offers his help and apparently his friendship as well, at least he insists on knowing Kraft's first name after introducing himself as Brad. Heart pounding, Kraft points to the most expensive model and in reply to Brad's question of which color he would like, he shrugs. *Take the silver one, Dick*, Brad advises, *that's the classic.* Kraft agrees, although he objects to a telephone being spoken of as a classic.

His relationship to digital progress—some even speak of a digital revolution, a concept Kraft rejects because as a rule in revolutions blood flows in the streets and men lose their heads, which, fortunately, one cannot say yet about what's happening here, apart, that is, from all those unhappy souls who end up under the wheels of a streetcar while staring at their smartphones or jump off the roof at Foxconn—Kraft's relationship to digital progress is, thus, an ambivalent one. At least that's the term he would use if anyone were to ask him about the apparent contradictions in his behavior, which, to his great astonishment, no one ever does. In public he likes to put up a front of disdainful scorn for the digital world and take every opportunity to stress how much it dabbles in formalism by throwing ever more refined and varied designs and distribution methods onto the market, kicking up a fair amount of mud in the process that in turn obscures—for those who are more easily blinded than Kraft—the fact that this oh-so-powerful revolution avoids almost all questions of content. No computer was necessary for the *Odyssey* to be written nor for Eschenbach's *Parzival*, or even Hölderlin's *Hyperion*, Kraft likes to argue, whereas it remains to be proven that a comparable masterpiece, shining brightly in the history of ideas, can be created in or despite the digital age and its tools. He is always ready to point out the superficiality of every manifestation of the digital, which he sees in a sharp contrast to the profundity of the enlightened mind.

On the other hand, he's an avid early adopter. Although he wrote both of his initial doctoral theses on a typeball electric typewriter he would wrap in a blanket on the back seat of his Ford Fiesta for the drives between Berlin and Basel, when it came to organizing the three thousand five hundred footnotes in his habilitation thesis, he used a Macintosh Plus, for which he'd had to take out a personal loan. He was also the first one in the university to parade the halls with a mobile telephone and he was filled with malicious glee when it rang in the middle of a faculty meeting, a tolling that to the other attendees sounded the decline of the West.

Kraft considers it his duty as a citizen to support the economy by acquiring electronic devices and he counters all skeptics by asking what society would otherwise do with all those young men from the south who, thanks to the phenomenal success of mobile telephones, show up in the most dismal pedestrian zones every morning, cheerful and motivated, their beards neatly trimmed, to fill the poorly paid positions offered by the mobile telephone stores.

In the back room, a glass-roofed cathedral, Kraft's heart breaks out in palpitations again when his credit card is swiped through the reader and Brad, visibly disappointed that their brief friendship is about to end, wishes him a lot of fun with his purchase.

Equipped with a new SIM card, Krafts sits in the shade of a green umbrella at Starbucks, logs on to the free Wi-Fi, and types his access code into the new phone. A raft of e-mails floods in, from his secretary in Tübingen, from a few students, from Heike, who wants to know if he's ordered their heating oil yet, it's not going to get any cheaper, and then the three most recent ones, all with the subject line *AlertSU*. The first, sent at 9:15 a.m., warns of an armed man on campus. Everyone is urgently advised to remain indoors and to stay away from windows. The second e-mail offers more detailed information: *At approximately 9:45 a.m., behind Cantor Arts Center, a male fired one shot into his head in what appears to be a suicide attempt. There is no threat to the Stanford community at this time.* A third, sent twenty minutes ago, lifts the alert, announces that the man had no connection to the university, and concludes with a long list of telephone numbers one can call in complete confidence in order to prevent one's own suicide or that of a fellow student.

Kraft finishes his coffee and heads back to campus, but when he sees the tower with all the books about war, revolution, and peace loom in front of him and thinks of the desk waiting for him on its ground floor, he sits down on the closely mown grass. Now that the chance of getting shot has disappeared and in light of the fact that

Tobias Erkner, the generous donor of the increasingly elusive million-dollar prize, has invited him to dinner, he desperately needs a complete intellectual and moral turn.

An intellectual and moral turn, like the one István and he had ardently called for—as they assured each other—long before Chancellor Helmut Kohl used just those terms in proclaiming a new era for the Federal Republic of Germany, but which they had completely forgotten about as a result of watching so much *Knight Rider*. All summer long they had clutched their pain, hatred, heartache, and self-pity tight, sunk side by side in the cushions of the sofa, from which position they let Michael Knight massage their souls and soften their brains. Their completely uncritical passion for a talking car and its pompadoured driver battling evil together can confidently be attributed to the fact that this enthusiasm was the one thing they could share in those trying hours and weeks—indeed, months, we must sadly admit. Self-pity, as a rule, is a difficult thing to share and only István suffered the ocular pain, just as he was the only one to feel hatred for the devious, gerbera-wielding attacker, hatred that seethed in him whenever he felt those stabs of pain and his bleary eye watered, soaking the bandage. No, Kraft could not share this hatred, even though his friend regularly enjoined him to, but in the end István's hatred and Kraft's heartache were focused on the same object, the broad-hipped, exceptionally maternal, peace-loving art student and enucleator Ruth Lambsdorff. This, however, was something his Hungarian friend was on no account to find out and so Kraft suffered in silence while István mostly whimpered faintly but from time to time broke out in loud Magyar curses before collapsing into an exhausted stupor.

chapter six

*Classical liberalism's confidence that the objectives of a
liberal society will be achieved through private enterprise
is only partially supported by historical experience. There
is no natural harmony between personal advantage
and the common good. [. . .] The tendency toward the
accumulation of private capital, visible in earnings from
interest returns and rising property values, is as much
a part of an economic system governed by the pursuit of
profit as the tendency toward the concentration of private
ownership of the means of production. They are the
reverse of the productivity ensured by the mechanisms of
such an economic system.*

*The free exercise of these negative tendencies in
unfettered productivity, will ultimately only destroy
its human element by always privileging the owner
over those who have nothing, the rich over the poor, the
producer over the consumer, capital over labor.*

—EXCERPT FROM THE FREE DEMOCRATIC PARTY'S
   FREIBURG THESES, 1971

ironically enough, it was a distant uncle of the object of their love and hatred who would rouse from their lethargy the two radical free marketeers busy licking their wounds, the aforementioned Count Otto Lambsdorff, federal minister for economic affairs for the Social-Liberal coalition, who presented his plan, "Manifesto for Market Economy: Concept for a Policy to Overcome Weak Growth Performance and Reduce Unemployment," on the 9th of September '82. Despite its technocratic title, this proposal filled them with the warmest emotions and set their hearts aflutter.

Thanks to his contacts in the Free Democratic Party, Kraft was able to get ahold of a copy of the document that same day and to celebrate the occasion, the young men went together to their hair salon of choice, where the owner, a pencil-thin old soldier with trembling hands who had learned his craft in the Wehrmacht, cut the hair close on the sides of their heads and shaved the napes of their necks with the assistance of a Bakelite clipper that clacked loudly when the motor was turned on, a sound Kraft associated more closely with solidity and dependability than any other sound in the world. All the while, he and István excitedly discussed the blue-blood recommendations in the FDP document in favor of cutting social services, read the most incisive passages aloud to each other, their voices cracking with exhilaration, and exclaimed for all to hear that Thatcher and Reagan's time had finally come in the Federal Republic as well, causing the clippers in the old barber's hands to shake even more violently, since all he could gather from this more or less incomprehensible conversation was that an Anglo-Saxon invasion of his homeland was imminent.

the following morning, they could hardly wait to get to the university, after having seriously neglected their studies for months. Freshly shaved and neatly combed, they knotted their striped ties, picked lint off each other's lapels, and polished their shoes; István wrapped his head in a clean bandage of a fresh yellow color that, Kraft assured him, differed only slightly from the official color of the Liberal Party. Thus accoutered, they made a triumphal entrance into the university and even the WOMEN ENRAGED that someone had graffitied with a thick brush on the rusted facade during their absence elicited nothing more than a scornful snort from István and a quick twitch of his bandage.

In front of the buildings they met groups of outraged students in a flurry of excitement, arguing and blowing the smoke from their hand-rolled cigarettes into the autumn air as if they were spitting in disgust. The word *betrayal* was being bandied about and there was talk of capitalist clear-cutting, of a declaration of war on the social state, but Kraft and Pánczél had a surprisingly hard time getting a foothold in the discussions. They had imagined they'd be attacked since they were known throughout the university as fiery advocates of an ultra-free market economic and libertarian social political system modeled on the Anglo-Saxon variety, as proponents of the very worldview that emanated from every line of the count's proposal, and they would have welcomed such attacks because they had so far simply not been taken seriously, their arguments striking their fellow students as too remote and eccentric. But now they would finally be in a position to stuff these simpletons' unwashed ears with evidence of their intellectual brilliance and worldly superiority, they assumed.

In this regard, however, Kraft and Pánczél were doubly deluded: on the one hand, there is no measurable or statistically verifiable connection between the cleanliness of one's ears and one's place on the political spectrum—István, of all people, should have refrained from such judgments at the time given that he had been limited to sponge baths since the 11th of June due to his eye injury, leaving his left ear hardly above corresponding suspicion—and on the other hand, none of the students had any desire to lend an ear to their intellectual brilliance, since they were all still too profoundly shocked at this betrayal by the Liberal Party to entertain the thought of a debate on the subject. To be sure, there were few supporters of Helmut Schmidt's government among the students, and hundreds of thousands of emphatic demonstrators were taking to the streets to protest the NATO Double-Track Decision that made provisions both for stationing new American nuclear missiles in Europe and for bilateral arms controls. But after fourteen years of the Social-Liberal coalition, most of the students had concluded that, under the circumstances, this coalition was the lesser evil and they had somehow ended up accepting the idea that the Liberals were a more or less trustworthy partner for the Social Democrats of the SPD. It was well-known that certain members of the FDP were flirting with radical economic liberalism, but the widespread hope had remained that the spirit that had guided German Liberals since the end of the 1960s, when they had adopted the Freiburg theses, which set the party in a direction supportive not only of the social state, but even of a reform of capitalism in order to achieve a government-controlled mechanism for greater distributive justice, would prevail. Now the Lambsdorff paper: betrayal! For the majority of the student body, solidarity with the Social Democrats was suddenly a kind of obligation and indignation was given free rein. It can come as no surprise, then, that no one wanted to deal with these two smirking fops, much less engage in an extended discussion of the subtle economic advantages of a supply-side versus a demand-driven economic policy. This may, however, also have had something to do with the fact that Kraft and Pánczél had well-formulated arguments at hand, supported by a frightening number of figures, statistics, and models they launched like a volley of arrow-headed footnotes. Their theoretical arsenal was terrifying and the frigid disregard for the less fortunate that emanated from the weapons they deployed inspired in their fellow students a premonition that a new time had come in which such brilliant but sadly socially inept misfits would have to be taken seriously. Still, for the moment the other students preferred to turn their backs on them and get worked up in like-minded company. Kraft and István were somewhat disappointed that their entry was not nearly as triumphal or controversial as they had hoped, but they sensed their time would soon come.

the situation escalated a few days later when Helmut Schmidt declared that the plan presented by his minister for economic affairs was tantamount to being served divorce papers. In response, the FDP foreign minister Genscher and three other Liberal cabinet members, including Count Lambsdorff, resigned. The coalition was thereby dissolved and the Liberals marched upon the enemy with flags waving and cries of joy from Grunewaldstraße. Kohl saw that the ideal opening for his intellectual and moral turn—which naturally could only be realized under his chancellorship—had come and he proposed a constructive vote of no confidence against the sitting chancellor.

The day before the big event, Kraft and István dressed to the nines and, giddy with anticipation, boarded the train to Cologne at Bahnhof Zoo. Yet when the train stopped at Griebnitzsee and the Transport Police, accompanied by a commando of German Democratic Republic ticket collectors, boarded the train, the shirt-washer Pánczél became noticeably quieter. Taciturn, he stared with his right eye at the actually existing socialism passing by the window. In his breast pocket burned a dark green passport with the Federal Republic's golden eagle, issued to a certain Gustl Knüttel, born in Neugablonz and now a pastry chef at the Kranzler. Thanks to his family's Bohemian roots, Knüttel was endowed with Eastern European features, which made his fiancée clap her hands in delight whenever István Pánczél pushed his tray up to her register in the student cafeteria of the Free University and exclaim that he, István, was the spitting image of Gustl. It was Kraft who came up with the idea that István should take advantage of his resemblance to said Gustl Knüttel and travel with his passport once it had become clear to them that flying was not an option due to budgetary constraints and they would therefore have to cross the territory of the workers' and farmers' state by train, exposing István to arrest by the German People's Police and the subsequent threat of extradition to the fellow socialist state of the Hungarian People's Republic. The pastry chef was persuaded to lend his pass by his fiancée, who in return for her support of this conspiratorial undertaking was loaned all the *Knight Rider* videos, which made her so happy she offered on the spot to blow out István's hair the way she styled Gustl's Bohemian locks so that the curly-haired István would be almost completely indistinguishable from the pastry chef, except for his cloudy eye, of course, but since it was so obviously a recent injury, it hardly had to be evident in the passport photo. It was, in fact, István's eye that got him through the passport control without a problem, because the officer, uncomfortable at the sight of the injury, had no wish to stare at the young man's sad face for any length of time, and so, happy to accept the rough resemblance between pastry chef Knüttel's passport photo and the shirt-washer Pánczél, he handed the false passport back without a word.

Thus the biggest danger was behind them, but the fear remained, and whenever the train slowed, István's complexion changed from ivory to ash gray and, his head pressed against the seat back, he kept repeating, "It's not going to stop, it's not going to stop . . ." At the border checkpoint in Marienborn, the train did come to a stop and tear after tear fell from Pánczél's eye and hung from his trembling chin . . .

Only once they reached Helmstedt did he relax, and for the entire stretch to Cologne, Pánczél tormented his fellow traveler with a detailed lecture on the foundations of game theory applied to the balance of fear, pausing only to offer asides praising the architectural qualities of the passing towns and the fashion sense of people on the train platforms at which their train stopped.

e arly on the morning of October 1, they left the youth hostel in Bonn and walked to the Parliament Building on the bank of the Rhine and found seats in the visitors' gallery of the assembly hall where they waited patiently for the members of parliament to arrive. Their sense that they were witnessing a significant historical event grew stronger when Hannelore Kohl and her two sons sat down near them.

Kraft's doubts that he was on the right side in the coming debate surfaced the moment Chancellor Schmidt stepped up to the podium wearing a dark three-piece suit and a thin silver-blue tie, his thick gray hair combed to one side, with exceptional statesmanlike aplomb— yes, Kraft even found his rasping chain-smoker's cough befitting a statesman—and opened the debate with admirable nonchalance, speaking of himself in the third person and making the planned unseating of the chancellor look like a revolution of dwarves incited by a corpulent giant. This man, Kraft was well aware, had the stature of a great head of state, and what fascinated Kraft even more was the sense of ease he emitted, the like of which, it seemed to Kraft, had never been seen in this country before. Schmidt addressed all the great men of this world as equals; he sat beside Carter with a broad smile, dynamic and decisive; next to Giscard d'Estaing he seemed a levelheaded intellectual, radiating esprit and charm; and his mere presence reduced Honecker to a little man in an oversize fur hat. In short, Kraft greatly regretted that they weren't on the same team.

Kraft's doubts were not assuaged by the performance of Rainer Barzel, who had to justify the vote of no-confidence for the opposition and displayed every bit as much self-confidence as the speaker before him, but none of the latter's elegance and natural nobility. He came off instead as an arrogant schoolyard bully who had been tasked by the teachers with overseeing recess. The chancellor meanwhile sat sprawled in an armchair behind the government bench, calmly snorting one pinch of snuff after another, managing to look as if he were slurping oysters. To be sure, the two men were well matched in arrogance, but while there was something coarse about Barzel's hubris, Schmidt seemed entitled to his.

Kraft gave his friend a sidelong glance to see if he was plagued by similar doubts, but István appeared intoxicated by the high mass of parliamentarian democracy and lapped up Barzel's every word as if it were sacramental wine transubstantiated to liberty.

It wasn't until the next speaker that Kraft was delivered from his doubts. It was easy for him to dismiss Wehner, the SPD parliamentary leader, as an old man, a dinosaur, an embodiment of that syndicalist clique prone to romantic ideas about society who were responsible, in Kraft's view, for the country's two million unemployed, and as someone who still acted as if most of the working class came home at night with machine oil on their hands or coal dust on their faces. The worst of it was that he seemed to believe it would always be so, whereas—and Kraft was sure of this—Germany had long ago set out on the irreversible path toward a service society; no, now there he had to correct himself, since he had learned from Thatcher that "there's no such thing as society," so Germany was rather on the path to a service . . . what exactly? . . . a loose collection of service individuals voluntarily aligned in family groups? It still wasn't entirely clear to Kraft what one could call the thing they lived in without using the term *society*. But Wehner's remarks tore Kraft from his reflections on the difficulties of conforming to correct Thatcherist vocabulary when the geezer, spraying old-man spittle over his papers, accused Count Lambsdorff of sinning against the younger generation. Kraft heard István gasping for breath beside him and before Kraft realized what he himself was doing, he shouted, "And what do you know of the younger generation?" into the rising wave of the Social Democrats' applause, loud enough for the president of the Bundestag, eyebrow raised, to give the visitors' gallery a stern look with a precautionary reach for the bell. Kraft ducked his head and muttered, "But it's true." Really, that old man couldn't read the signs of the times, and besides he had a tie the size of a rag around his neck that hung down his chest like a baby's bib.

In this respect, at least, the next speaker scored some points: Mischnick's tie won Kraft's approval even if the Liberal parliamentary leader himself didn't have a shred of Helmut Schmidt's elegance and ease. And it didn't help that he began his speech by emphasizing what a difficult period Germany had entered, what a difficult time it was for this parliament too, and finally what a difficult time it was for him personally. Stuff and nonsense, Kraft muttered, in what way is this such a difficult time? It was an opportunity for a nation standing on the brink of disaster, that's what it was. It was time to air out the social-democratic fug, cut taxes, shrink the state, deregulate the banks, privatize the railroads, the post office, the telephone, electricity; out with Keynes, in with Friedman and Hayek; free the individual from the state's stranglehold; consolidate the national budget; relax labor laws; reduce maternity benefits, federal training assistance, and housing subsidies, or better yet, eliminate them altogether. *Liberty, liberty*, the word buzzed in Kraft's head.

This Mischnick, however, was much too hesitant, too soft, too prudent, even if, as Kraft had to admit, his well-formulated phrases, his refusal to sweep away all doubt, the way he measured his words, had a certain charm and, from an intellectual point of view, were certainly preferable to the ranting of a Barzel. Still, Kraft had traveled to Bonn to witness a final showdown and a crushing victory, so he applauded wildly when Mischnick overcame his restraint and raised his voice in a call to abandon the entitlement mentality, jabbing his index finger at the podium to underscore each and every word as if he were squashing an entire tribe of beetles.

When the ex-chancellor Willy Brandt took his place at the podium as chairman of the Social Democratic Party, István stood up and announced, looking to the right and left to appraise the effect of his words, that he was not willing to listen to this man who had knelt down, who had prostrated himself in the dirt before the communists, no, he, István, having suffered under that system, did not have to put up with this, no one had the right to demand it of him, and he strode toward the exit with an expression of scorn. Kraft sank into his seat, his ears burning with shame, and let his companion leave. The significance of Brandt's genuflection in Warsaw was one of the few points on which they had never been able to agree. Kraft had a vivid memory of sitting in front of the television as a twelve-year-old and watching the man who now stood at the podium sink to his knees in a dark coat and kneel silently with hands joined for a half minute and the boy had a strong intuition that this gesture of humility had something to do with his father, an SS officer and leader of an Einsatzgruppe who was taken prisoner by the Soviets in the summer of '41 on the western shore of Lake Peipus and spent the next fourteen years in a prison camp in Arkhangelsk before he was finally released in the fall of 1955 with the very last prisoners and mistakenly taken by the Red Cross not to Hamburg but to Munich, where he seized the opportunity to make up for the fourteen lost years and, even though he set an impressive pace in every other respect, it took him a full two years to decide to look in on his wife in Hamburg, a young woman he had married on his first leave but returned to find as a childless spinster who'd waited for him all those years in her garret apartment, which didn't prevent him from conceiving a son with her before disappearing for good three days later. Richard Kraft, who had inherited nothing from his father aside from his family name, gray eyes, and curly hair, and who, because of his sketchy knowledge of history, didn't know how to interpret the chancellor's gesture at the time, and so succumbed to the mistaken notion at the sight of the kneeling man that the latter was asking Kraft's pardon for his father's absence, and indeed because he was a child as thirsty for knowledge as he was solitary, he wanted to understand the situation better, so with his savings he bought a copy of *Der Spiegel* with a picture of the kneeling chancellor on the cover. A reporter who had witnessed the scene in Warsaw recounted it with emotion: *He kneels down not for his own sake.* The boy felt somehow validated. He'd had a sense that the chancellor was not kneeling down for himself, no, he was kneeling for the boy's father, but reading further he no longer understood what the reporter was writing about. *He, someone who need not kneel, kneels for all those who should be there on their knees, but are not—because they do not dare or cannot or cannot dare kneel. Thus he acknowledges a burden of guilt which he himself does not bear, and he asks for forgiveness which he himself does not need. He kneels for Germany.* What guilt was this? And why was this chancellor not part of that Germany that was guilty and therefore someone who did not need to kneel? And what about Kraft's father? Was he someone who should be kneeling, and was it because he wasn't that the chancellor had to? Kraft had no one who could give him any answers, but he knew where answers could be found, so he went to look for them in the public library, which turned out to be a complicated endeavor since the league of German historians had up to that point neglected to devote themselves to the subject of guilt with due scholarly rigor. Kraft found answers in the novels of Seghers, Grass, and Becker, and in Celan's poetry and Bachmann's stories.

The chancellor, Kraft learned, actually *had* fallen to his knees on behalf of his father and had also fallen to his knees for him, the son, since the sins of the fathers and the iniquity of the entire country were so abysmal that they were visited on all sons like a hereditary illness. And so it was the gesture of humility made by this old man standing at the podium that had politicized Kraft and awoken his interest in history and literature.

Brandt spoke for a long time, a very long time, and despite the fact that the man meant a great deal to him, Kraft was about to get up and join his friend in the lobby, but then the debate heated up, indeed, there was veritable turmoil in the auditorium after the recently ousted ex-minister Baum had spoken. István had returned to his seat for the speech and had immediately denied Baum's right to call himself a liberal after he, now a simple member of parliament, had voiced his confidence in the current chancellor, proof that he completely misunderstood the true liberal spirit and was fundamentally unfit to take the sacred word *liberty* in his putrid mouth; a verdict with which Kraft eagerly concurred, happy to reestablish harmony with his friend.

Then Dr. Hamm-Brücher, a tall, elegant woman in a severe black-and-white-striped skirt suit and a tie-neck blouse with her snow-white hair pinned up, denounced her own party's attempted putsch as the opprobrium of democratic decency, a remark István scornfully dismissed as whining prattle, besides, she reminded him of his grandmother, who reminded him in turn of his mother, and that said it all. Kraft wasn't sure what exactly that said, but he secretly wished Dr. Hamm-Brücher reminded him of his mother, which was not even remotely the case, as Josephine Kraft probably had no idea what "opprobrium" was and in any case she'd never shown the slightest interest in "democratic decency" nor owned an elegant skirt suit.

The secretary-general of the Christian Democratic Union, who followed this distinguished figure, condemned her words as an attack on the constitution, inciting a commotion. At any rate, the CDU man's provocation didn't lack for effect and Kraft had the pleasure of enjoying one last appearance by Chancellor Schmidt, who proved his statesmanliness once again when, interrupted from the floor, he shouted that for the time being he still had the right to speak. István gaped at the theatrics, filled with delight. Kraft felt a certain amount of unease, but suppressed it and tried to share in his friend's enjoyment; yet when, at last, the prospective chancellor stood at the podium, trying to mask the clumsiness of his appearance, his thinking, and his language with dynamic gestures, Kraft suddenly felt as if he had eaten too much of some heavy peasant dish and, even worse, that he would be served nothing but such heavy fare for a long time to come.

On the trip home, the Hungarian student Pánczél dreamed of rockets, of Pershing, and of cruise missiles aimed at his former homeland. Now that the timid SPD, infiltrated by naïfs from the peace movement, had been relegated to the opposition and the libertarians could push around the newly anointed Christian Democratic chancellor, it was just a matter of time until the Americans were allowed to station their recently developed Pershing II and cruise missiles in the Federal Republic. István had studied the technology of the new weapons in depth and had become convinced that a new chapter in the annals of nuclear strategy had begun and that, as a result, the prospect of world annihilation, which he found interesting at least with regard to certain game-theory considerations, was not now an inevitability but simply one of two extant possibilities because these much more precise new weapons could execute surgical strikes that would excise the tumor of communism from the healthy body of the nation, an option he envisioned as a scenario in which the Széchenyi thermal baths in Budapest, or more exactly, the outdoor pool framed by the baths' florid neo-baroque architecture, played a central role: In István's fantasy, the central pool was filled with the portly bodies of the socialist cadres, dipping their short peckers in the sulfurous water and patting each other on their hairy backs. Then he would launch one of those splendid rockets, armed with an atomic warhead. From Bavaria it would skim the treetops, fly over Salzburg, covering the breadth of Austria at a furious pace and crossing the Hungarian border under the radar, then it would detonate exactly in the central pool of the Széchenyi thermal baths. Neutron bomb: a clean solution. The architecture he admires remains intact but the water in the sky-blue basin boils, the Party officials who had been smirking a moment before sit screaming in the simmering brew, shreds of their skin already floating on the bubbling surface, a giant cloud of steam rises from the pool and slowly drifts away. A dry basin remains with the motionless red bodies of the despicable brood lying like boiled crabs on the bottom of the pool, while outside the baths, outside the radius of this targeted blast, the common people are already getting heroically back on their feet. This was the scenario he played out in his mind again and again, enriched with new details each time, that helped him endure his return through passport control and the zone and brought a rapturous smile to his lips despite the tracts of socialist desolation outside the train window.

Kraft let him dream. He himself was downright taciturn since leaving the Parliament Building. After more than five hours of debate, the motion was finally put to a vote, and Kraft, feeling exhausted, had left the visitors' gallery to smoke a cigarette outside, while István watched every single one of the 495 members of parliament walk up to the ballot box and cast his or her vote. Shortly after 3:00 p.m., the president of the Bundestag announced the tally, then addressed Deputy Kohl and asked if he was willing to accept his election to the presidency. *Mister President, I accept the election*, Kohl replied, stretching to his full height, whereas Schmidt sat immobile as a statue among the members of his group before finally rising to congratulate his opponent. But it wasn't this gesture that impressed Kraft the most, rather it was what he noticed in a brief sidelong glance at Kohl's family. Hannelore Kohl had not applauded, she had not smiled, she had merely stared impassively at the massive back of her husband, who was now chancellor of the Federal Republic. Their sons, young men in blue suits, sat motionless beside her. One bit his lips, the other shook his head slightly in disbelief, and for a brief moment twisted his mouth beneath the down of his nascent mustache into a bitter, ironic smile.

Kraft would very much have liked to have known what knowledge provoked this reaction in the young man. Gazing out into the autumn landscape of Saxony-Anhalt, he recalled the young man's face and imagined him saying to himself, *That's all we needed*, and to the members of parliament, *You'll soon see what you've gotten yourselves into*. Kraft worried that at the very moment of their patriarch's greatest triumph, the entire Kohl family had withheld their confidence that his character was suitable for the office he had just attained.

Kraft's worries soon proved to be not entirely unfounded. The promised intellectual and moral turn never came. By and large Kohl's government followed Helmut Schmidt's program, albeit without his elegance. The count's plan, which had so enthralled our two young freethinkers, disappeared into a drawer and was only dug up again twenty years later by, ironically enough, a social-democratic government. The economic liberals remained junior partners just as they had been in the old coalition. Neither Reaganomics nor Thatcherism found their way into the Federal Republic. The NATO Double-Track Decision was, indeed, implemented, and István got his missiles, but their deployment expanded the peace movement's ranks to unexpected numbers and led to the rise of a new party that struck Kraft and István as suspicious and frivolous. In the end, it wasn't

Kohl's character that proved to be the real problem; it was, rather, his inadequate intellect, which tormented them deeply and led them to agree on the view of his election as an operational glitch in democracy that would soon be corrected: a misapprehension, as the next sixteen years would show.

*t*his much, however, is certain: a turn was effected on the Grunewaldstraße sofa. The *Knight Rider* videocassettes remained with Gustl Knüttel's fiancée, the ironing board and the shoe-shine box experienced a period of intense activity, and the two friends dove into their studies with élan and enthusiasm.

The wounds Ruth had inflicted on Kraft healed and in the spring he had recovered sufficiently to blather with amorous intent—seated at a cafeteria table in a Basel pharmaceutical company that had put its auditorium at the disposal of a seminar financed by the Mont Pèlerin Society for the younger generations of Europe's economic liberals, to which he and István had been invited—at a doctoral student in biology from Lörrach doing research on the genetics of yeast in the pharmaceutical company's laboratory; even though, as a wistful Kraft had to admit, her hips were hardly of Lambsdorffian dimensions.

chapter seven

I'm gonna have to science the shit out of this!

—MARK WATNEY

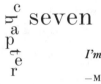raft stands up, brushes the grass from the seat of his pants, and slinks back to the tower with a heavy heart. He tacks across the lobby and sneaks into the reading room behind the back of a security guard in a red jacket. He can already hear the vacuum cleaner in the distance and, feeling as if it's sucking the last bit of life force from his body, he can't keep from his mind the image of Heike

unwrapping a chicken breast from the butcher paper and, because of her fear of germs—one of the few things they still share—using an appliance purchased for just this purpose to suck all the air out of the storage bag so that the plastic seals itself tightly around the meat. Kraft feels his own chest tighten.

He quickly packs up his things, escapes the coolness of the reading room, and goes outdoors, where everything is as usual. Latinos weed the flower beds on their knees, professors hurry to lectures and seminars in black Reebok classics, sand-colored chinos, and plaid button-down shirts, and all around him is a throng of calves, thick and thin, hairy and silky smooth, muscular and anorexic, male and female legs, all of them in shorts and most of them pedaling; a repugnant parade of legs, Kraft finds, all the more so as most of them, to make matters even worse, display their bare feet in flip-flops, although only very few feet are worthy of being shown. With regard to feet, Kraft is strict and fastidious. In fact, as far as he's concerned, male or female, they all belong clad in solid and elegant and certainly well-kept shoes, all of them hidden from sight unless it's a question of baby feet, then he's willing to make an exception, or if one happens to be engaged in an interaction of a sexual nature with the feet's owner, then in such cases, yes, in such cases Kraft is oddly enough able, albeit only in those rare moments when he can really let himself go, to thrill at the sight of feet and lick and suck on them with quiet passion and considerable stamina; in better days, he even used to nibble occasionally on Heike's bunions with a mixture of tenderness and unbridled desire. But at the moment, he would rather not think of his girls' baby feet or Heike's bunions, so he pictures one of the students exuberantly cycling past slipping off the pedals because of his completely inappropriate footwear and getting his toes caught in the glittering spokes. With that, Kraft loses control of his imagination and conjures up a complete bloodbath, lets the student with half-severed toes crash for good measure, cracking his gleaming white teeth, which leads to a massive pileup of dozens of bicycles colliding and young bodies hurtling onto the hot pavement with shrieks of pain, gashing open their flawless knees, scraping their taut thighs, and, here they have only themselves to blame, twisting their ankles terribly in their idiotic flip-flops, so that Kraft believes he can even hear the pop of snapping ligaments.

It is hardly surprising then, that a few minutes later he stands feeling queasy and indecisive in front of the lunch buffet in the Arbuckle Dining Pavilion, leaves the grilled turkey legs and burritos untouched, hesitates over the sushi as well, and finally serves himself a small helping from the salad bar. Carrying a few leaves of iceberg lettuce crowned with four pale strips of chicken breast and a dollop of Thousand Island dressing along with a can of Diet Coke, he looks for a free table in the Knight Management Center courtyard, which, as Ivan has explained to him, was generously endowed with several hundred million dollars by Nike co-founder and Stanford business school graduate Phil Knight, and because there are no free tables, he asks two young men if he can join them. They have no objection and continue their conversation without paying him any attention. While he pokes desultorily at his salad, pushes the chicken breast to the edge of his plate, and swipes at the screen of his new gadget, he can't help but overhear the loud conversation at his table and soon he is listening closely, only pretending to look at his phone.

It's been a good year, one of them says, a great year, fantastic. He has a square jaw, as big as a night-table drawer, out of which gleam an extravagant number of teeth. I'm doing well, I'm doing well, he repeats again and again. And his tablemate, a curly-haired young man in a light blue dress shirt replies: Good for you, bro, good for you, you deserve it. Kraft has the impression that he is sincere and genuinely pleased for his friend. The square jaw of the man in the pink polo shirt glows with a smile that rivals the California sun, but then his smooth-shaven face suddenly darkens. He's still bothered by the fact that he's not able to measure his success precisely. Here, too, his friend seems completely in sync and dons an expression of profound dissatisfaction. It is, indeed, an immensely frustrating problem that keeps him up at night, too. From the rest of the conversation, Kraft gathers that this difficult problem will one day solve itself when they enter the phase of earning money because then key parameters will be at hand and direct comparisons easily made. But in the current phase, it's agonizing that there are no measures available to calibrate your own success. It might be worth developing an app for that, Curly Hair muses, folding his pizza slice in two, it's worth considering. For a moment, Kraft has trouble following the conversation. There's talk of algorithms to be developed, of implementation, resiliencies, and parameters, of input and output, of scales and the reduction of complexity, but Kraft is pretty sure they're still talking about a way to precisely measure Square Jaw's success. He finds this bewildering. Naturally, when he was their age, he also thought a lot about his success and how it compared to this or that person's, but it soon became clear to him that it was a question that couldn't be answered because success never came without its mirror image. There is always the success others attribute to you and the success you attribute to yourself and the more you try to bring them into alignment, the more obvious it becomes that you have no idea how successful other people think you are. This is something you will never know because you have to factor in lies, malice, and envy, and that's precisely why the only thing you can do is rely on your own feelings, and these swing wildly, as Kraft has understood since puberty, between self-loathing and delusions of grandeur.

To think these two halfwits actually believe they could tackle this fundamental aporia with an app. Deluded, Kraft thinks, quantitatively deluded.

The two men sigh at the immensity of the task and shake their heads atop their broad necks. In any case, the one with the extravagant number of teeth rushes to say, as if he couldn't bear to linger on even the thought of failure, he's raised his productivity over the last two months. He points to a kind of oversize sippy cup filled with an unappetizing viscous grayish-brown liquid. Nine thousand two hundred sixty-one minutes, he says after checking his phone, that's how much time he's saved thanks to Soylent. At this news, Curly Hair puts the slice of pizza, from which he had been about to take a bite, back on his plate and whistles through his teeth; 9,261 minutes, that's 154.35 hours or 6.43 days, impressive, very impressive. What Kraft finds most impressive is how quickly the young man did the calculations. Math-cretin, he thinks, idiot, autist. Square Jaw grabs his giant sippy cup, takes a swig, and with his cheeks full, he lets the liquid trickle down his throat for a moment before gulping loudly. Kraft stares at his remarkably prominent Adam's apple as it bounces and thinks of cats and mice with a faint sense of superiority, convinced the two number crunchers wouldn't grasp the subtle literary allusion.

The thought of 6.43 days in a bottle, that piques his curiosity after all. What had they called the brew: Soylent? The word sparks a faint memory. He googles discreetly while he listens to Curly Hair justify the slice of pizza on his plate. It's primarily the taste of melted cheese he can't do without, maybe because of his Italian ancestry, eating was always central to family life at home, and he can certainly imagine that if he were of Irish ancestry like his interlocutor, he'd have an easier time switching to Soylent. This is a claim his friend rejects and asserts that he, too, hasn't completely given up recreational food, he eats out once a week, usually on social occasions. Recreational food? Kraft can't believe his ears.

Here it is, he found it. Soylent is apparently a brand of liquid meal replacement products, not one of those horrible diet drinks Ruth consumed for a while after she had weaned her second child and mistakenly tried to pin her unhappiness on her figure, no, Soylent is seen as a long-term replacement for normal food and an intelligent alternative to the usual "rotting ingredients," as the inventor of the grayish-brown goo calls traditional food. *Food wastes more than just our time*, Kraft reads on the screen of his phone. Eating is a widely overrated, extremely labor-intensive, and uneconomical activity; grocery shopping is a nuisance; and the preparation of traditional meals is a waste of time and an inefficient use of resources. That is why, the inventor of Soylent explains, he decided to devote his life to reproducing food empirically. Kraft shivers. This, then, is the future. No, even worse, it's the present: you take a human activity—in this case, eating— isolate it from all cultural significance, all historical connections, all emotional ballast until nothing but the bare essentials are left. The brew in the sippy cup is the quantifiable remains of a rich and influential cultural activity developed over thousands of years dissolved into a series of measured values: so many grams of protein, so many grams of fat, 0.03 grams of this vitamin, one iota of that trace element, etc., etc. But what worries Kraft most is the realization that behind this process of quantification lies a longing for optimization through rationalization: nothing other than maximizing the product by minimizing the cost, in this case by saving time. And this, Kraft knows well, is nothing other than the fundamental calculation of capitalism. Why, then, does the sippy cup inspire such dread in Kraft? Shouldn't it serve as proof of the robustness of his own convictions?

He catches himself recoiling yet again as he does each time he stumbles upon a concrete, practical example of something that is undeniably a real-life consequence of the theories he's spent his life thinking through and defending. This has been happening more often of late. On top of it all, he has to admit that although the guy on the other side of the table has been subsisting solely on this slop for two months, he looks outrageously healthy, sitting there with his splayed legs and his powerful jaw, farting unselfconsciously in the California heat as if it were the most natural thing in the world.

It suddenly occurs to Kraft where he's heard the name before. *Soylent Green*, that was the title of a dystopian science-fiction movie from the '70s; an overpopulated world, food shortages, the government feeds the people with protein wafers and in the midst of it all Charlton Heston is tracking down a dark secret. Kraft can remember the final scene in which a dying Heston is being carried off on a stretcher and with his last ounce of strength he shouts, "Soylent green is made out of people!" Is this brand name the expression of a strange sense of humor, or, as Kraft supposes, does the inventor think the idea of making foodstuff out of dead people is less outlandish than simply economical? This is a possibility that should at least be considered, since death itself could be subject to a process of quantification by isolating it from all cultural, historical, and emotional connotations and exposing its measurable, corporeal core. What remains is the calorific value of the human body. Kraft recalls a study with the wonderful title "The Limited Nutritional Value of Cannibalism" he had come upon in an old issue of *American Anthropologist*. The authors came to the conclusion that a skillfully butchered fifty-kilo man delivers the minimum daily ration of protein for sixty men of roughly the same weight. "One man, in other words, serves 60, skimpily."

"Excuse me?" the two young men ask in unison, and turn to Kraft with inquisitive expressions. Kraft realizes he must have said the last sentence aloud and as the blood rushes to his head, he apologizes, he was just thinking out loud, there was a banquet, a birthday dinner for a colleague he had to organize, and he was just wondering how many waiters he would need to hire. The two men turn to face him and Kraft gathers from their demeanor that, amazingly enough, they seem genuinely interested in his problem and are ready to talk it over with him. "Sit-down dinner or flying buffet?" the melted-cheese lover wants to know. "Never mind," Kraft says, afraid the other one is about to suggest serving the dinner guests giant sippy cups of Soylent and he's in no mood to get caught up in a discussion that would no doubt require using the concept of "recreational food," which he feared would molder in his mouth like fungus and leave a stale aftertaste in revenge, a risk that was not worth taking, especially since he had just then invented the topic in a panic.

But he knows he won't escape that easily and so takes an offensive tack and asks if they're students at the Stanford business school. To Kraft's relief, they're happy to reply. They are graduates but are working on their start-ups in an incubator associated with the university, an unbelievably inspiring place where Stanford's best minds and most audacious entrepreneurs meet and are provided contact with the most important investors and the best mentors in the world. You can find a lot of "disruptive energy" there, an expression Kraft finds as irritating as his own irritation at feeling irritated, because he wasn't born yesterday and so is of course aware of the current enthusiasm for the idea of disruption, having read about it in countless articles and studies and subjected it to theoretical analysis in heated seminar discussions. He had even smoothed its sharp edges to integrate it seamlessly into his own thinking, but now, hearing it spoken of with such sincere enthusiasm and unqualified approval, he finds it threatening.

The young man with the curly hair starts talking passionately about his start-up, which he's just successfully steered through a first round of financing, with its app, called Famethrower, already well into beta. Basically, he explains, it's a range accelerator for live video-stream services like Periscope, Meerkat, or Facebook Live. Kraft unfortunately has to admit that he doesn't know those apps and doesn't really have any idea what a live video stream is. They're only too happy to explain it all to him and as an example the broad-jawed one shows him an app on his iPhone featuring a world map covered with red and blue dots. Now Kraft has to tell them where he's from and the young man zooms in to southern Germany and right away, without needing the search function, he finds Tübingen, calling it "Hölderlin's town," and his colleague adds that the poet lived and studied there with Hegel and Schelling. And don't forget, the first one interjects, Friedrich Miescher discovered nucleic acid in pus cells there in 1869. Kraft, feeling rather intimidated at this point, feigns a lively interest. Not much going on in Tübingen these days, the broad-jawed one says regretfully, and taps on one of the three red dots on the Neckar River. After loading for a few seconds, an intimate scene appears on the screen. Two girls, thirteen or fourteen years old, Kraft guesses, are sitting on a bed. One of them brushes her friend's thick, dark hair while she, in turn, seems to be holding up her phone and filming herself and her friend. The girls are talking casually and easily about a girl in their school in the slang of young Eastern European immigrants. The transmission quality is impressive; Kraft notices how chipped the red nail polish is on the hand pulling the brush again and again through the gleaming hair. Behind them, on the wall of this girl's bedroom in Tübingen, is a poster of Nicki Minaj's monumental rear end, a sight Kraft knows all too well, since every time he enters the twins' room, he is subjected to the hypnotic power those gigantic buttocks exert on him, a pull that is almost as strong as

Rumsfeld's piercing gaze. Even his daughters had noticed he had trouble tearing his eyes away from their poster and took advantage of the opportunity to embarrass him.

Espalier pear tree, he'd murmured, and fled. Every time he sees the pink thong that disappears between the sumptuous mounds of flesh just below the coccyx, he can't help but think of the espalier pear tree in his grandfather's garden that climbed up the wall of the house on tautly strung wires. He had only visited his grandfather in Altes Land once, he and his mother, and while she was talking to her father, a man whose face Kraft could not recall, he was sent out to the shady garden, where he shivered in his thin jacket and stood in the only patch of sun, his face to the wall, enjoying the warmth on his back. Right in front of his face, nature had refused to be tamed by the steel wire; the pear tree's gnarled wood had incorporated the wire into a thick knot divided in two. A single drop of resin gleamed in the sealed crack. The taut wire disappeared into this growth like the pink string between Nicki Minaj's fleshy buttocks, into which the stretchy synthetic string—Kraft was certain it was elastic because in his imagination he had plucked at it to make sure—seemed to have permanently grown. On the way home, his mother was unfamiliarly cheerful, almost girlish and willing to be silly. In Hamburg, she bought him a warmer jacket and, in a Nordsee restaurant, they ate breaded cod fillets with tartar sauce.

Espalier pear, espalier pear. Kraft lets these words circle in his mind like a calming mantra to keep from punching the broad jaw as punishment for dragging him without a word of warning into this intimate scene, into this girl's room ten thousand kilometers away, where neither he nor the two young men have any business being. Is that live? he asks, aghast. Absolutely, it's happening right now, at this very second, on the other side of the world. Can they see us? Kraft wants to know. No, they can't but we can send them a message and with baboonish speed he types *Hi Girrrls, what's up? Like your hiar! Hair!!!;)!!!* on his screen. A fraction of a second later, Kraft hears a light pling in the girls' room in Tübingen and sees one of the girls raise her eyes to the camera and echo the sentence that had just been typed in California. She purses her lips and blows a kiss. The melted-cheese lover reacts by frenetically typing on his phone and generating a roundelay of colorful little hearts that dance across the screen.

And that's your invention? Kraft asks, dumbfounded. No, no, unfortunately not, the young man regrets, Periscope was developed by two colleagues who sold the app to Twitter for tens of millions of dollars. There are a handful of similar services, but his app, Famethrower, is a platform that brings all these services together and solves a huge problem they all share. You see, he says, our two Tübingen girls only have five people watching despite the gleaming hair. Isn't that unfair? And yet, reach is everything, at least from the point of view of the one posting. For those watching, on the other hand, it's essential to be able to filter out relevant data from ten thousand live-streams being broadcast on the internet around the world at any given time. His app meets both needs. A complex algorithm, the center-piece of his start-up, calculates relevance by evaluating a multitude of parameters. Facial recognition software with access to all the large image databases, social networks, and short message services identifies in a fraction of a second who can be seen on any given livestream. If you were standing in front of Justin Bieber in line at a Starbucks and streamed yourself with Bieber in the background, your relevance value would rise suddenly because Bieber is one of the most prominent and active users of social networks and short message services, so Famethrower would recommend this stream to its users as especially worth watching. Not only that, this software can also identify

2,127 different human and animal activities as well as several million landmarks. So not only is it important who is doing something, but also what they're doing and where. If, for example, Justin Bieber showed signs of being drunk, this software would evaluate the live-stream as more important than if he were just waiting in line. Bieber throwing up, his friend adds, would be a real boost in terms of relevance. Kraft has a strong urge to argue with them about the concept of relevance, but he keeps it in check and continues listening to their enthusiastic explanations.

Brushing hair is about in the middle of the relevance scale, brushing another person's hair is a bit higher and studies have shown that an astonishing number of men have a hair-brushing fetish. The software, Kraft is told in a whisper, can learn. AI, the other one adds as if this acronym bathed everything it was applied to with the nimbus of a bright future. The software searches the internet independently for the latest news, the most popular hashtags, and the most frequently used search terms, so it's able to constantly reevaluate the relevance of people, activities, and places. On top of that, it learns from its users because they can pick Famestars by double-tapping on the screen, and this raises the livestream broadcast in the rankings, or, conversely, they can give "Wrinkles" to a stream they don't like and when enough people have done this and the livestream looks old and crumpled, it falls in the rankings. The app is still in the development stage, but the beta version is already pretty satisfactory. Unfortunately, at this stage, it's unable to distinguish between real people and two-dimensional images, so the Tübingen girls' stream would be near the top of the rankings right now because the software would combine mutual hair-brushing by underage girls with face-sitting, thanks to Nicki Minaj. These, however, are just the usual childhood diseases the developers will be eradicating in the coming weeks. Maybe he'd like to be a beta tester? And before Kraft can decline the offer, he's urged to photograph the QR code on the young man's screen with his own phone. Kraft, who suddenly has a splitting headache, does what he's told, obediently pushes accept, and watches as Famethrower is installed on his new iPhone along with a half-dozen livestreaming apps.

On the way home, surrounded by all these young people whose flawless bodies suddenly seem so gentle, so vulnerable, and infinitely worth protecting, he is ashamed of the bloodbath he had fantasized earlier. He wants to safeguard them all, to form a protective shell with his hands and carry them to safety like robin redbreast chicks—or purple finches, for all he cares—that have fallen from the nest. Why this sudden fit of tenderness? It certainly wouldn't be unfair to assume that his concern wasn't actually for the Stanford students on their bicycles, but instead for his daughters in Tübingen, whose vulnerability had just been demonstrated in both a general and a very concrete way. However, because he knows, or more exactly, refuses to admit that his worry for his daughters is nothing more than a cheap sentiment as long as he's here fighting for the prize that will relieve him of his fatherly obligations—thanks, no less, to the vulgar power of money—he prefers to focus his concern on these teenagers he doesn't know from Adam.

Whatever you do, don't think of little-girl feet now!

But, dear Kraft—as one would like to call to him—can't you see, right here, the tip of an idea that could save you if you only tugged on it? Who could object if you recognized in your worry for your daughters the real reason you haven't been able to rise to the challenge of the contest with your usual brilliance? You fundamentally don't want to win this prize because you know it would be wrong. That's how it is, isn't it? Come on, Kraft, this is your straw: grab it!

But no, Kraft can't trick himself so easily into grabbing this straw. Because he knows that's simply not the way it is. *Nothing is ever that simple, not ever!* he hears as a distant cry. This was a lesson he had to learn early. For example, when his mother's lighthearted cheer had completely vanished the day after their visit to his grandfather and she started an argument with him over some triviality, maybe because he had left his shoes in the small entryway. She berated the young Richard until he began to cry and then kept at him until he began to rage against the injustice being perpetrated upon him, and once he began to rage, she took his new jacket back to the department store in punishment. Yes, that's when it first dawned on him that nothing is ever simple. Not ever! And every single line he read in the public library in his effort to understand why someone who did not need to kneel would kneel for his father confirmed this intuition.

And so he wasn't surprised then that the question of freedom also turned out to be complicated. Kraft and Pánczél argued for freedom with the combined forces of their intellects and yet were met only with incomprehension by their fellow students, the result, quite simply, of the fact that they all felt quite free already, whereas Kraft and István, in their fury, appeared anything but free. Besides, and this was completely obvious, they were in a tough spot for their crusade—in West Berlin . . . at the Free University . . . in the early 1980s. They were like refrigerator salesmen in Greenland.

Why then, since Kraft understood all this—unlike István, who didn't seem to appreciate the context—why then didn't he just relax and enjoy the freedom he had? Because that was no longer possible. He was a seer, he had perceived the nature of things in their irreducible complexity, but his insight was not of the kind that would have allowed him to don the priestly robe of purity and unambiguity that promises inward peace. Quite the contrary, he had fully grasped that there is nothing outside of history, that nothing and above all no one possesses an immutable nature. He knew that nothing is ever simple, not ever. He was lost for all eternity.

He could not simply deny this. That would mean intentionally abandoning his knowledge, and this was an act he was utterly incapable of committing; it would merely have led him into a new kind of misery because, in the circumstances, knowledge was all that was left to him. He had known for a long time that there was no escape for him, but he had developed a tactic—as long as you talked about things, you still had a chance. As long as you were busy describing something, as long as you were still developing your ideas, as long as you were offering arguments pro and contra, as long as you were drawing conclusions and weren't bothered with the fact that on closer examination your premises turned out to be less than clear, then things were still undecided and had not yet come to their inevitable, always inexplicable and unbearably contradictory and vague end. This is why Kraft talked and argued incessantly, why he always disagreed and tried to formulate a more precise description than what had come before; this is why the young Kraft—and, we have to admit, sometimes the older Kraft too—was a blatherer. As long as you were talking, things remained simple—why did no one seem to understand this except for him?

It was this exceptionalism that widened the distance that had set in between Kraft and Pánczél in the months after the chancellor's ouster in Bonn and was reinforced by their disappointment at the fizzling of the so-called turn. Their great, unconditional love was over, the love that had driven Schlüti, the third wheel, crazy at first and then finally out of the Grunewaldstraße flat. As before, they still stood side by side in their fight for liberty and against big government, in support of nuclear deterrence, low taxes, personal responsibility, investment incentives, and privatization—but they began dividing up their tasks.

István focused on questions of defense policy and strategic studies, especially of the nuclear variety, in other words, on that branch of science he referred to, with a dramatic roll of his one good eye, as the *Strangelovian Sciences*, a little ironic joke that he failed to notice nearly upset the balance of terror among his fellow students, even though, by then, they should have been used to his rhetoric.

István thus became representative of that strange species who called themselves "defense intellectuals" to differentiate themselves from the dim-witted generals whose twitching index fingers were forever hovering over the red button. In doing so, István subordinated his thought completely to the Cold War rationality, which differed in several essential ways from all the other rationalities to which humanity had hitherto committed itself, first and foremost, namely, in the fact that it was seen as perfectly reasonable to always take into account the complete annihilation of humanity, the *ultimum malum*, so to speak, which had the terrifying effect of making talk of the ultima ratio seem entirely mundane. As a result, the experts, among whom István now counted himself, constantly had to point out that there was a fundamental, even transcendental difference between the ultima ratio regum, the final resort of kings, which phrase Cardinal Richelieu had engraved on the barrels of cannons during the Thirty Years' War, and the discretionary power of a handful of heads of state and party leaders over their nuclear arsenal. But because this ultimate evil that could be visited on an entire species through the decision of one single man now existed and had been brought into existence with the assistance of the natural sciences, these defense intellectuals were convinced that it was possible to control it using methods developed by those same natural sciences, and therefore took pains to keep their strategic thought strictly formal and independent of any particular individual or context, that is, to rely on algorithms that functioned as a set of inflexible rules and would lead to a necessary solution. By separating out all cultural and historical connotations together with their peculiarities, the most optimistic of the defense intellectuals hoped the rules could be applied mechanically and all decisions be left to computers.

Which is why István was convinced that this rationality would prevail over simple reason and thus serve as a guarantee for peace. With the conviction of a prophet, he harangued his fellow students, especially the female ones, and, deploying his well-stocked and detailed knowledge, he presented thoughts based on game theory, carried on about first- and second-strike capabilities, the Nash equilibrium, and the nuclear triad; he weighed megatons against megadeaths, and spoke easily of unspeakable things, until the opposition had no alternative but to shout *Petting statt Pershing!** an argument István countered by saying he didn't see what was wrong with *Petting AND Pershing*, besides the fact that, in bed, he was a regular long-range missile and always ready to prove this. Kraft, who had witnessed many of these encounters, feared for István's other eye each and every time.

Kraft devoted himself entirely to discussions of supply-side economic policies and told everyone willing to listen—and even those who weren't—how best to handle the sharp-edged implements of investment incentives: deregulation, privatization, and tax reduction. A drastic Anglo-Saxon remedy straight out of Margaret Thatcher's handbag, a remedy that, naturally, nations could only afford if they kept their public-spending ratio to a minimum and took a scythe to

---

* "Petting not Pershing!"—*petting* as in making out; *Pershing* as in the American-made Pershing II nuclear missiles based in Germany.

welfare assistance. Laissez-faire, laissez-faire . . . , Kraft liked to repeat in a worldly tone, feeling like a rebel. Deep down he was an anarchist, a punk, he would say to himself, but with a higher level of hygiene, better taste, and good manners . . . All bullshit, as he knew perfectly well; it wasn't that simple, nothing was, and besides which, his reputation as a man with a heart of stone beating under his perfectly pressed shirt, a consequence of his political opinions, bothered him. In the meantime, he no longer found it particularly appealing to be considered the most promising of all the promising students on account of his eccentricity, because he had come to realize that it only made him attractive to a very small group of women, who were much too eccentric for his own basic tastes, which is why, since Ruth Lambsdorff's rejection, he had developed a vain craving for admiration that now prompted him at every opportunity—citing Reagan's young budget director as his authority—to extol trickle-down theory, which is essentially a synonym for supply-side economics and demonstrates that when prosperity is poured over the top economic performers with a watering can, it will trickle down to the less prosperous and ultimately improve everyone's lot, simultaneously demonstrating that reproaching economic liberalism as coldhearted is completely unfair, because it's clear that it is, in truth, a profoundly social project. This splendid mechanism has been known since the days of Adam Smith, and Kraft just doesn't get why so many people refuse to understand it despite the simple beauty of this physics-based metaphor, vividly reinforced by daily experience when water from the showerhead pours down on their heads, flows down their bodies, and pools around their toes. Maybe Kraft would have better understood his interlocutors' apparent obtuseness if he had deigned to read the works of J. K. Galbraith, the leftist economic liberal and proponent of demand-side economics who had pointed out that, when he was young, trickle-down theory was known as the "horseshit theory": "If you feed the horse enough oats, some will pass through to the road for the sparrows." But Kraft didn't read that sort of book, which is why he sang the praises of the prosperity that would soon fall on everyone like a warm tropical rain from the seventh heaven of the free market, and why he was soon known throughout the Free University as the *rainmaker*, which, in turn, understandably, ran against the grain of his craving for admiration; it wasn't simple . . . nothing was . . . no, not simple at all.

eight

An analysis of other ergosterol mother liquors for the
preparation of a new base material was in progress
when we were forced to interrupt our work in the state
just described following the complete destruction of
all material in an air raid.

—HILDEGARD HAMM-BRÜCHER

nor was anything simple with Johanna, the doctoral student in biology whom Kraft had approached in the cafeteria of a Basel pharmaceutical company with the words *and love never ends*, grinning conspiratorially at her over his plate on which grilled slices of banana and canned pineapple chunks swam with strips of turkey breast in a bright yellow sauce surrounded by a ring of rice. Not surprisingly, this provoked no small level of irritation in the young woman, which feeling required a considerable amount of energy and a nearly endless flood of words from Kraft to defray, since she didn't know this romantic vow was the epigraph of Ödön von Horváth's Oktoberfest play *Kasimir and Karoline*, and Kraft was equally clueless that the dish the cafeteria cook had recommended to him as Rice Kasimir with the rasping *K* of the region was actually called Rice Casimir and therefore—but certainly for other reasons as well—he had a lot of explaining to do, and their first conversation was, accordingly, very confused.

No, nothing was simple with her either. And not only because their first exchange was a difficult one. Kraft was lucky in that Johanna never stayed irritated for long, she didn't have the time, and we can assume that by the end of their first meeting she had already forgotten its strange beginning even though this initial encounter only lasted as long as it took to shovel the rice dish into her skinny body with the help of a spoon she held in her fist as if she had only just learned how to eat with silverware the day before. She was sorry, she told Kraft, wiping her mouth with the back of her hand, she had to get back to her yeasts, but he could wait for her outside laboratory building B at quarter past nine.

Kraft had no idea what to expect when they met at the arranged time and place and so imagined a whole range of possibilities and, having arrived at laboratory building B fifteen minutes early, he had time enough to wonder which part of their brief lunchtime conversation could possibly have induced Johanna to want to see him again; a mystery he would never even come close to solving.

At quarter past nine on the dot, Johanna appeared on the stairs in a white lab coat that hung loosely from her narrow shoulders. This outfit puzzled Kraft because it didn't fit any of the scenarios he had imagined, but Johanna had no intention of going anywhere with him. She just wanted to smoke a few cigarettes with Kraft right there, outside the door, before going back to her strains of yeast. And that's exactly what happened. Kraft didn't even try to persuade her to hang her coat up and leave her sac fungi in their petri dishes to their own devices for a few hours—in other words, to their tireless asexual reproduction and the transformation of sugar into alcohol, so that the two of them could pursue similar ends, that is, to turning alcohol into sugar and giddiness before devoting themselves to sexual reproduction. But no, they did what Johanna had intended, the first instance of a pattern of behavior that would define their relationship.

Kraft smoked two cigarettes as Johanna smoked three, each facing the other and saying almost nothing since she had the habit of smoking like a Calabrian street paver with the cigarette wedged in the left corner of her mouth, which allowed her to rub her always cold hands together but at the same time considerably hampered any conversation. Kraft was briefly tempted to remark on the meteorological phenomenon causing the cold snap they were suffering and its designation as a *Schafskälte* or "sheep's cold snap," about which he had just read a clever commentary in *Die Zeit*, but he had the feeling Johanna wasn't interested in commentary, so instead he stared silently at the growing worm of ash on the end of her cigarette, which gradually bent toward the ground and eventually fell right onto her canvas shoes, completely unnoticed by Johanna and without dirtying her lab coat, which in turn drew his attention once again to her body's apparently deficient motherliness. For a painful moment he thought of Ruth and how, even though he had never seen her smoke, she would have brushed cigarette ash from her opulent bosom with an energetic gesture. Johanna stamped out her last cigarette, took three steps toward Kraft, and, while he was struck by the faint smell of freshly opened champagne coming from her short hair, he felt her cold hands on his neck, pulling downward as she rose onto her tiptoes.

But it wasn't the memory of this kiss, which left him somewhat confused and with a persistent erection, that ultimately prompted him to undertake the long train ride from Berlin back to Basel two weeks later, taking Johanna up on the invitation she had extended after licking her lips and before disappearing into laboratory building B. He should come back the weekend after next, she had said over her shoulder, when she'd have concluded a series of experiments and would have more time.

Over the following days, Kraft spent many hours on the Grunewaldstraße sofa, mulling over her offer. What made him hesitate wasn't the lack of anything maternal about Johanna; she was no Ruth Lambsdorff, that was true, but the alluring contrast between her decisive manner and her delicate body, her short-cropped hair, and her fine, almost boyish features at least caught his interest. István, whose advice he had sought, concluded, once Kraft had assured him that she was definitely not a communist, but seemed, instead, to have no interest at all in politics, that there was nothing to think about: her kiss pointed to only one conclusion, that a weekend with her promised to be a satisfying experience well worth the cost of the train ticket. But for a long time, Kraft was still not sure he should make the trip because he couldn't imagine what she wanted from him or what she saw in him. And for Kraft, that was a remarkable question. A completely new question, an unheard-of question. Not once had he asked himself—unlike we, ourselves—what Ruth had wanted from him or saw in him, preoccupied as he had been with what he wanted.

It would be easy to assume that Kraft had learned something from the debacle with Ruth and evidently become a better person, or at least a better man, but here too things just weren't that simple, and to do justice to Kraft—at least the Kraft of those days—we have to admit that this simply wasn't so—not at all—even if this means rejecting an edifying narrative, that of the young man who has learned a lesson in humility and who tries from then on to see beyond the horizon of his own sensitivities, even if this, in turn, puts Kraft in a far from flattering light. We must, therefore, also take into account the possibility that his efforts to find out what Johanna wanted from him had little to do with finding out anything about Johanna, and much more with finding out something about himself; a very obvious possibility if we consider that at the time Kraft was prepared to embrace contingency with an entirely new fervor and to banish his craving for security and clarity to the deepest recesses of his unconscious, which, of course, caused it to surface all the more vehemently and manifestly in his consciousness, only to be denied and repressed anew in a self-reinforcing feedback loop. It was thus a profoundly unsettled, even downright unhinged Kraft, a Kraft on a quest, who set out early for the long journey to Basel two Saturdays later and embarked on the return journey even more unsettled and unhinged at noon on the Sunday.

He had not found an answer, but István's prognosis at least proved correct; the kiss was a promise Johanna kept without hesitation and in roughly the same way as she ate: voraciously, avidly, insatiably. She grabbed the spoon in her fist, so to speak, took stains on fabrics in stride, and, most gratifyingly, didn't give a damn about good manners at table or in bed. Nonetheless—and this is a clear sign of how thoroughly unhinged Kraft was—by the time he arrived at Bahnhof Zoo on Sunday night, Kraft wasn't sure if it had really been worth the cost of the train ticket since he was no closer to the answer he was so desperately seeking.

At first his impending exams kept him from brooding. On Monday morning he found a seat in the university's reading room and started studying. In the afternoons, around three, he'd be overcome with hunger and against the rules would secretly take bites from yeast rolls he'd smuggled into the library. Pretending he was looking for something under the table, he would stick his nose deep into the bag from the bakery and the scent would set off echoes of his night with Johanna, which would in turn spark a sudden desire for maternal love and an equally sudden libidinous desire that led him to search the library's shelves and leaf through the clips in the Munzinger Archive with clammy fingers, looking for Hildegard Hamm-Brücher's biography. In his despair and in violation of his principles, Kraft was immediately inclined to interpret as an omen the fact that this elegant woman who had so impressed him the previous autumn with her use of the term *opprobrium* had written her thesis on the mother liquors of yeast in the technical extraction of ergosterol. The yeast researcher Johanna was the one for him, he decided, and he was able to think himself so thoroughly into this love that he was replete with it when, two weeks later, he stood outside laboratory building B again, waiting for Johanna and then, his heart racing, was able to confess this love to her. Johanna put her cold hands soothingly on his burning ears and said, but of course, Richard, we love each other, and for her that was enough said on the topic for years to come.

Although the yeasts had been the indirect agents of their love, they were nonetheless by and large the source of not inconsiderable difficulty. On the one hand, they left Johanna little time for her private life and Kraft always had to compete for what little free time she had, which she devoted, and here he couldn't complain, reliably and exclusively to him, and when they were together she was always completely present. All the same, Kraft occasionally suspected her of using the extensive care her yeasts required and their fragility as a cover story and he felt it would be more honest of her to admit that she had a level of interest in her work that she could not summon for him. In any case, she rarely visited him in Berlin and so it was Kraft who undertook the long journey as often as possible, and this put an enormous strain on his budget—which consisted solely of his stipend from the Friedrich Naumann Foundation—and put further distance between him and István.

Johanna's relationship with her yeasts, on the other hand, was utterly uncomplicated, marked by a steadfast scientific pragmatism and supported by clear questions she directed at her single-celled organisms and the equally clear answers she received in return. She moved, she was told by a Kraft who knew every trick in the book of the philosophy of science, entirely within the narrow limits of a paradigm and was therefore still in that "normal science" phase, which genetics had meanwhile also reached, and so was busy solving puzzles. Johanna took note of this description impassively, to Kraft's disappointment, since he had meant it as a provocation. Kraft envied her for being so comfortably and unquestioningly at home in her "thought collective" and its "thought style" and for simply doing her work in perfect methodical and theoretical accord, with passion but completely free of any epistemological doubt. Her assurance, in contrast to his present hesitancy, made him feel even less self-assured and so it was rather an act of defiance when he decided, after completing his master's in economics—a degree he received, true to form, with distinction, and despite an attractive thesis project proposed by one of his professors—to devote himself entirely to his minor fields of study, of which there were more than enough, what with German literature, philosophy, political science, sociology, and history, thus forgoing the opportunity to enter the fold of a field that claimed to be an exact science, a claim Kraft had in any case never accepted even though his public insistence on specific theories might have led to the opposite conclusion. But at least, and this we must keep in mind, he could have had a brilliant career in economics. Beginning, no doubt, with a painless Ph.D. thesis, and then, his name preceded by the title of doctor, he could have taken up a mid-level position in a large bank or insurance company and rocketed to the head of the business; the only problem was that Kraft had too little interest in money, had never had any interest, really. Instead, he decided to pursue an ambitious double doctorate in German literature and philosophy.

The fox, as he had read in an essay by Isaiah Berlin, who was quoting a fragment by Archilochus, knows many things but the hedgehog one big thing and Kraft found this essay so comforting that he chose the difference between the fox's knowledge and that of a hedgehog as the topic of his dissertation at the Free University. From the very first sentences, he was on familiar territory again in the great intellectual historian's skeptical thinking—conveniently enough also appreciated by Margaret Thatcher—since Berlin believed Archilochus's enigmatic sentence about the hedgehog and the fox could easily be understood to mean that the fox, for all his cunning, is no match for the one defense of the hedgehog, a defense that was, at least in Kraft's view, repellently straightforward. However, because things are never simple—again, in Kraft's own interpretation—the sentence could also be understood quite differently to mean that thinking human beings could be divided roughly into two categories, into hedgehogs and foxes: the hedgehogs are those who subordinate the entirety of their thought to a single, universal, organizing principle and thus adhere to a system that alone gives significance to all that they are and say, whereas the foxes refuse to subordinate their thought to a system and instead, free-floating, they seize upon the essence of a vast variety of experiences and objects for what they are in themselves, without any hope of finding one unchanging, all-embracing whole, free of contradictions. There exists a great chasm between these two kinds of human beings, Kraft read in Berlin's essay, and he agreed with all his heart. Yes, indeed, and he, Kraft was undeniably a fox, and it would be his task, he was convinced, to bring serious and scientifically rigorous support to that intellectual fidibus, Berlin—that is, to delineate the chasm historically and buttress it with a watertight epistemological foundation—but over the following years it became clear that this endeavor was more difficult than he'd anticipated, because Isaiah Berlin didn't actually need his support, and furthermore, Kraft pursued this endeavor, as he himself had to admit, with growing frustration and despair, like a hedgehog-in-chief, by trying to systematically demonstrate the fox's unsystematic thought. It also didn't help that Kraft was essentially following a hidden agenda in that he wasn't merely trying to establish objectively the difference between hedgehogs and foxes, far from it, but wanted above all to demonstrate that the latter were somehow more clear-sighted in their perception of the true essence of things; and that, in itself, was a rather hedgehog-like thing to do.

He had no such difficulties with his German literature dissertation, which he had begun working on in parallel at the University of Basel so as to have a good reason to spend more time with Johanna. He completed his thorough if rather conventional study of Ernst Jünger's poetics without agony except for the time it was the spark of his first real fight with Johanna, when he read passages from *On the Marble Cliffs* to her in bed in a solemn voice and she broke out in laughter and refused to believe that Jünger had meant any of it seriously.

Despite such occasional irritations and although Kraft never did find out what Johanna saw in him, they endured each other for four years. In the good moments, Johanna gave him a sense of security. In the bad ones, she made him feel even more insecure.

a nd then, Kraft thinks, when he watches the first lights of the city emerge, then I made her so furious she disappeared to San Francisco for good.

chapter nine

*The man was all wind . . . Oh no! If only it had been
wind; instead it was a blowing vacuum.*

—GEORG CHRISTOPH LICHTENBERG

kraft feels the security glass, cool and hard, against
his temple. When he closes his eyes the endless
chain of red taillights seeps into the darkness in his
skull. It is quiet in Ivan's car. They have hardly spoken since
they left Stanford. In stops and starts interrupted by excruciat-
ing moments of complete immobility, they creep through the
luminous valley in their capsule of metal, glass, and worn leather.

Ivan drums his fingers on the steering wheel.

Less than twenty-four hours have passed since Kraft, stark naked, with the damp soil of the marshlands under his feet, broke down at the sight of these lights, overcome with a vague sense of guilt.

In the ten days that he's been in Silicon Valley, Kraft has easily managed to avoid visiting San Francisco. After all, he had work to do in the library, work that became more and more urgent with each passing day of idleness, and a visit to Fog City . . . No, no, he had no time for that. But today he could no longer avoid it. Tobias Erkner had invited them, flashing his million dollars, so Ivan and Kraft climbed into the SUV in the early evening and joined the line of programmers, techies, and entrepreneurs heading home.

A silence separates them. They've hardly been alone together for more than a minute since the first evening of Kraft's visit, when they sat across from each other over red wine and chocolate cake, and they haven't recovered any of the closeness they shared in the days when they cheered the leader of the free world on his first visit to Berlin. Instead, a sense of awkwardness fills the space between them. Kraft takes a sidelong look at his friend. They're no longer twenty, that's true, and that kind of friendship, Kraft knows, is no longer an option for men of their age; only those whose lives have as yet been relatively humiliation free can still believe that having a friend they can share everything with is a beautiful thing. But still, Kraft remembers, when Johanna disappeared, István was the one who helped him recover from his state of confusion and self-dissolution, and if Kraft were someone generous enough to recognize the important contributions others make to one's own biography, then this would be the proper moment to acknowledge that no other person has had as great an influence on his life as the shirt-washer Pánczél. But Kraft is not a generous man, never was. Not out of hard-heartedness. No, but because he sees himself, and always has, as someone who doesn't have much to give others. And that's why he is suddenly flooded with a strong emotion and has to turn away quickly and stare out his window. If we were sitting in the back seat right now, we would catch them both wiping away a tear, one automatically, the other furtively.

After Johanna, carrying two giant, heavy suitcases, slammed the door behind her—which, we must assume, she only did in Kraft's memory of the event, because we'd like to hear him explain how exactly a woman as delicate as Johanna could slam a door with a suitcase in each hand—Kraft had fled to István in London, who was studying at the London School of Economics and Political Science to make a name for himself as a nuclear strategist thanks to a stipend from a stinking-rich Hungarian who had emigrated to America yet retained a soft spot for Eastern European dissidents. Kraft arrived in London in an advanced state of breakdown and took over the sofa in István's kitchen. Years of insecurity had worn him down, four years of feeling inferior to Johanna, years during which he never did find out what she actually saw in him or what she wanted from him, a period during which he envied her work in the natural sciences, four years during which the ground had swayed under his feet, during which all his beautiful intellectual constructs began to show cracks and flaws as soon as he built them and large chunks of their lovely plasterwork fell to the ground. Kraft, stretched out on István's sofa, was the survivor of an earthquake.

For four years he had tried to prove that the fox's way of contemplating the world was the reasonable one and he became more and more of a hedgehog in the process, fighting against this transformation so forcefully that he lacerated himself with his own spines. What made him most insecure was that no one seemed to notice this but him. He had failed in his own eyes; his doctoral thesis was a patch-up job, underpinned by a system in which he himself had so little confidence that he spread it out in all directions and welded onto it any number of reinforcements and pointless rivets to disguise any resemblance to a system he found so repugnant. He had plastered it with his stupendous knowledge of the relevant secondary literature and in a final show of strength had applied the varnish of rhetoric that was apparently eloquent enough to win the praise of the professors at the Free University, and even a commendation. You hedgehog, thought Kraft when the dean handed him his diploma in front of the festively dressed audience. He accepted it with a hint of a bow and joined the circle of Erinaceidae with a smile of resignation. Although he wasn't yet thirty, Kraft was tired of the battle. So be it, he'd be a hedgehog. Trying to be a fox exhausted him. Nothing was simple, not ever. He had talked himself hoarse and racked his brains. He longed for solid ground, longed to only have to know one thing on which all else was based, to which everything was related.

Disheartened and abandoned by Johanna, Kraft buried his face in the brown cushions that smelled of rancid fat on István's sofa and hoped sleep would console him.

But that's not what happened. István didn't let him sleep. Kraft's Hungarian friend was full of energy, he had settled himself comfortably in the promised land of Margaret Thatcher, was living his dream of real existing economic libertarianism, as he called it, was passionate about his studies and bursting with an optimism Kraft could not escape. István would not accept his friend's capitulation. Sure, nothing was ever simple, and hedgehogs were wrong, but occasionally rightness and wrongness weren't relevant, as István never failed to remind his friend, because you simply have to make a political point. If it's a matter of defending freedom, then there's no room for doubt, and all you need is a *Here I stand, I can do no other.* And when István saw that his friend was still not entirely convinced and still longed for eternal sleep, he explained to Kraft that true foxes—which is what the two of them indisputably were—well, among all the things true foxes know is also the one thing the hedgehogs know and the only thing foxes don't know: that is, what it feels like to be a hedgehog. Even so, it doesn't mean that they aren't able, when necessary, to behave like hedgehogs: to turn their backs on the world and bristle their rhetorical quills.

A fox with quills? A porcupine? Kraft asked doubtfully. But the longer he considered the idea, the better he liked it. A porcupine, yes, maybe that was the solution, you could escape contingency and find refuge in the knowledge of facts, and if that wasn't enough, there was always discourse, and if you doubted your own words too much, then you had recourse to self-defense and could retreat to a firm stance from which you could overlook the fact that nothing is simple. Kraft found new hope and they sat fraternally side by side on the sofa just as they had on Grunewaldstraße, and turned on the television. It was June 12, 1987, and Reagan was visiting Berlin for the second time. This time they'd set up his podium in front of the Brandenburg Gate. Amazingly, the president looked almost as jaunty as he had that summer five years earlier. Seated to his right was unfortunately no longer the elegant Schmidt, but the massive Kohl, who prompted a snort of disgust from István, because the chancellor had completely fallen from István's favor when he was reported to have said he feared the British prime minister like the devil fears holy water. As well he should, as well he should, was István's retort. Relaxed, Kraft listened to the speech, happy not to have to stand in a crowd of flag-wavers. And when, at the end of his speech, Reagan directly addressed the demonstrators, who once again filled the streets of Berlin in great number, István jumped up in outrage and accused Reagan of plagiarism. Kraft was grateful to his friend and in a conciliatory mood, so he neglected to point out that he couldn't remember seeing an agent following them on bicycle down Ahornallee, trench coat flapping, but instead nodded in agreement to István's great delight.

again Ivan drummed his fingers lightly on the steering wheel. Kraft looked intently out of the passenger-side window. They were never again as close as they were on István's brown London sofa. He'd like to share this memory with Ivan, but he doesn't dare. It's his memory, not Ivan's, and besides, right now, Ivan looks like he's somewhere else completely.

Kraft left London after a few days. Back in Berlin, full of István's contagious optimism, he plunged into his work: a postdoctoral thesis on the sublime, decked out with so many historical details, and indeed an overabundance of factual knowledge, that it swelled to three volumes and assured its author, through sheer weight, stupendous scholarly virtuosity, and 3,500 footnotes, a secure place in the landscape of German thinkers, making it just a matter of time before Herr Professor Dr. Dr. Kraft would command a prestigious professorial chair.

ivan exits the highway and they drive through a residential area, up a perfectly straight, steep street, over the top of a hill with a view of the city and the bay, and down again, past small wooden houses. This is Kraft's first time in San Francisco, but it's one of those places whose strong presence in pop culture has left such a thick sediment of cinematic and literary images in his memory that he now feels the wildly contradictory emotions of returning to a well-known place and of entering uncharted territory overlap, and with the knowledge that Johanna lives somewhere in these hills, it gives rise to a distant echo of the confusion he suffered over their years together. A confusion whose inception he associates with the ironic smirk under the sparse blond mustache of the chancellor's son and whose end he feels was marked by Reagan's second visit to Berlin. He'd thought he had left this confusion behind long ago, had shut it out of his life with a solid wall of ideas, reinforced with battlements of persuasion and a broad moat brimming with knowledge. Only seldom, very seldom, did the distant, unsettling cry reach him over the parapets: *It's not that simple, Kraft, nothing ever is.* But generally, the cry was soft enough for Kraft to ignore it.

erkner is waiting for them on the corner of Valencia and Twenty-First, accompanied by a young woman who is introduced as Gwen Ives and who beams at them with wide open eyes as if she had been waiting her entire life to meet them. Kraft, caught off guard by so much warmth, also widens his eyes, tries to show a few teeth, and watches in irritation as Ivan hands her the car keys and thoughtlessly turns his back on her. Gwen is apparently only there to spare them the inconvenience of looking for a parking spot because Kraft doesn't see her again until hours later on the other side of the city when she drives up in Ivan's car with a beaming smile and looks deep into Kraft's eyes as if she had thought of nothing and no one but him the entire time. Maybe, Kraft thinks, Gwen was not hired merely to spare her boss the trouble of parking, but also to offer his guests an appropriate dose of eye contact. Erkner is not one for eye contact. Not that he seems unfriendly or insecure. Quite the contrary, he stands up straight, shoulders back, in a slim tailor-made suit that reveals a fair amount of his well-toned, tanned chest; he speaks loudly and without stumbling or hesitating, yet not once does he meet the eye of the person he is speaking to. Often Erkner keeps his eyes fixed on a distant point just over Kraft's shoulder then quickly sweeps them over his face as if they were skidding, and steadies them again over his other shoulder, so that all evening Kraft has the unpleasant feeling that something is happening behind him that is more worthy of Erkner's attention.

Erkner's telephone vibrates and after a brief glance at the screen he tells them they need to hurry because the restaurant unfortunately has a strict first-come-first-serve policy and doesn't take reservations, and his assistant who's been waiting in line has almost reached the door.

The line in front of the restaurant called THE MAC&CHEESE stretches halfway down the block. Erkner hurries along the line and stops near the front next to a young man who waved at him from a distance and whom Erkner now greets with such an ostentatious show of friendship that Kraft has the impression the slight young man has stiffened under the hail of backslapping. This is Eddie, Eddie Willers, a deeply valued colleague. At these words, Eddie nervously adjusts his horn-rimmed glasses and blushes. The entire scene seems staged to Kraft, but what does he know about the social behavior of multimillionaire Silicon Valley investors, and in any case he has little time to think about the topic since they are quickly joined by another young man, with a shaved head, meaty cauliflower ears, and a blond goatee braided into a rattail that dangles decoratively over the kaffiyeh wrapped around his thick neck. Aside from the goatee and the kerchief, Ragnar Danneskjöld isn't wearing much: a black MIT wrestling singlet, Roman sandals, and a Rolex Deepsea, which Kraft, interested in mechanical wristwatches ever since Heike had given him a restored Milgauss for his fiftieth birthday, registers with a connoisseur's eye.

Ragnar, as Erkner explains, is the founder and director of the ThunderXStruck Institute, one of his many investments and one particularly close to his heart even if it won't show a profit for the foreseeable future. This is because it's a project to develop the Sea Steadies, artificial islands outside of all territorial waters and out of reach of regulations, ineffective governments, and messy politics, which will function as laboratories and breeding grounds for new forms of free cohabitation. Kraft pictures an island like those he's seen in cartoons of castaways, a tiny island of sand with a single palm tree and a horde of sunburned young men and women indulging in an orgy, but he already senses that Erkner's investment in a free future has less to do with free love and sexual exchanges than free trade and monetary transactions. Ragnar starts to elaborate on his vision but his élan is brought up short by a man in a rustic leather apron like those worn by artisans who have devoted their lives to crafts that are threatened with extinction, and this aproned man leads them into the restaurant to a booth paneled in blond wood.

Diners are spared the chore of choosing what they'd like to eat. There's only one dish on the menu. Erkner orders five portions and a round of beer that the waitress brings to their table. They solicit Kraft's expertise in his capacity as a German and he is grateful to Ragnar for explaining in detail the origin of the bottle's contents, which owes its particular aroma to the Russian River's singular climatic conditions, about which he knows a thing or two, because this gives Kraft the time to rummage through his memory for the English word for "hoppy," which absolutely eludes him. He is saved by a small procession of leather aprons carrying five redwood boards, each bearing a cast-iron pan filled with spätzle. At a loss, Kraft examines the noodle gratin topped with golden-brown bread crumbs with cheese sauce bubbling around its edges, but it seems there won't be enough time for anything this evening, certainly not for wondering, because the waiter launches into an explanation of the ingredients in the dish, underpinned by elegant hand gestures, that begins with praise for the tubular pasta, made exclusively with spring water and organic wheat from the foothills of the Sierra Nevada and shaped in copper molds, followed by a lengthy excursus on the three types of cheese used this evening, a Blue Fog Mountain from Humboldt County, an applewood smoked cheddar from Sonoma Valley, and finally a mozzarella made with the milk of Simmental cows who enjoy a view of the Pacific from Point Reyes day in and day out, and whose milk, furthermore, is as exceptionally full-flavored as it is extraordinarily digestible. Then, with a flourish, the waiter pulls a long grater out of a bamboo sheath and, to top it all off, he planes a few shavings of cave-aged Jack over each of the party's bread crumbs, exuding as much enthusiasm as Ragnar, who takes advantage of the moment to draw Kraft's attention to the grater, which was forged by an old Japanese man in Big Sur from fifty layers of Damascus steel. This, Erkner proclaims, is *the ultimate mac and cheese*, the chef here has raised this dish to a whole new level, from zero straight to one, so to speak.

Kraft watches Ragnar raise an overflowing forkful of the steaming dish to his mouth, shovel the bubbling mass into his cheek pouches, adorning his beard with cheesy tinsel in the process, chew rapidly, breathing in gasps all the while to cool the inside of his mouth and blowing his fiery exhalations over the table, then shovel more loads into his gullet. For all that, Ragnar still manages, at the request of Erkner—who, for his part spoons the simmering children's food into his mouth with mechanical precision, unaffected by the heat, whereas Kraft feels his soft palate contract with the very first forkful like a plastic bag thrown into the fire—to present an overview of his institute and the work being done there, which, if Kraft understands the man in the wrestling singlet's plan correctly, consists of saving the world by building, with the support of Tobias Erkner's many millions, a large number of floating islands they intend to anchor in international waters, that is, outside of any national jurisdiction, so they can devote themselves communally, unhindered by government regulations and spared the trouble of convincing those too thick to understand, to work, to business, and last but not least, to the development of new models of society, which, freed from the rotten sediment left by hundreds of thousands of years of politics, could thrive in fresh, unspoiled, and above all controllable ground, like hothouse tomatoes in the pure, germ-free substrate of digital technology, and if a community does not develop in a direction you deem acceptable, you can achieve ultimate freedom by decoupling your part of the island—the plan is to build the Sea Steadies according to a modular system adapted from the process of evolution—and set sail over the open seas in search of a new community you can dock with, which allows you, en passant, to consign to the archives of history the rigid concept of nationality as lifelong obligation, that straitjacket and breeding ground of nationalism. Ragnar underscores this point by picking a few strands of cheese from his goatee and rolling them between thumb and index finger into a tiny ball, which he tosses into his maw after the last forkful of macaroni and cheese, all of which suggests to Kraft that simply being able to set sail would, in fact, be a great advantage, but Kraft doesn't have a chance to develop this thought because Ragnar Danneskjöld, picking up speed, launches into a description of what he calls the "Cambrian explosion of *governance*": with the abandonment of the old, land-based rules that take the joy out of life, millions will be catapulted out of poverty through the construction of one Singapore or Hong Kong after another and, at the same time, furthermore—and he marks his enumeration by jabbing his fork, on the tines of which a single noodle is impaled, into the air—diseases will be eradicated, the oceans cleaned, carbon dioxide filtered out of the atmosphere, the world fed, and fossil fuels replaced by algae, but all of this, the man in the kaffiyeh affirms as he scrapes the cheese crust from the edge of his pan, can only happen if people pull up stakes and make a new land their own, expand the frontier yet again, because peaceful evolution, unlike perpetually bloody revolution, can only occur in new niches, and after all, it's not only the individual species that evolve, no, cultures are subject to evolution as well, even systems of government develop according to Darwinian principles but only as long as there is room for new concepts, for example, direct democracy, organized through social networks and managed without legislative power, or a community that ratifies its own rules and laws and formulates them according to the participatory principles of the open-source movement in a kind of Legipedia, or even—and why not—enterprises that offer flat rates for all services, well-designed and user-friendly products that until now have been offered by the state, so that you could change providers when dissatisfied, in short, it's time to colonize the oceans; these dynamic systems would offer dynamic, fluid individuals—*pioneers with new notions for new nations*, as Ragnar waxed alliterative—the opportunity for evolution without revolution.

Ragnar sets down his fork and looks expectantly at his interlocutor. Kraft doesn't know what to say. Erkner jumps in and explains that there are a hundred million people around the world who are ready to leave their homeland and set out in search of a better life. Now Kraft has even less idea what to say. How is he supposed to equate the millions of Africans, Afghanis, and Iraqis with rudimentary educations who are crossing the desert in trucks and on foot and who are venturing across the Mediterranean in overloaded inflatable boats so they can pick tomatoes in European hothouses with Ragnar's high-tech vision of floating *work-life habitats* in a Jonathan Ive–like design for digital nomads with degrees from universities that jockey for the top ten places on ShanghaiRanking? But who knows, maybe he's being too pessimistic? In any case, Erkner is prepared to invest his millions in the project and maybe he, Kraft, is just an old fossil, too rigid to appreciate the beauty of the notion. He certainly doesn't want to come off as a cultural pessimist and critic of technology, not today, not in front of Erkner, whose prize money must be won through optimism, so he asks with a show of interest how far the project has advanced, confident that he will hear astonishing things about gigantic, modular, self-sufficient island structures on the open sea, on which the first settlers are already busy cultivating algae and disruption.

And what he hears is, indeed, astonishing: they're about to anchor a few old pontoons that have been welded together in the San Francisco Bay, not far from Oakland, on which they'll install *work-life habitats* made out of containers. The first community is expected to move in next summer. This description sounds to Kraft more like one of those run-down boats turned into discos that are tied up along the bank of the Neckar, or those dreary accommodations for asylum seekers in the Hamburg port. At least this allows him to connect Ragnar's brave new world to the Africans whose sandals made from old tires are left stuck on the razor wire of the fences around Ceuta and Melilla, but the discrepancy between what they envision and what they've achieved seems to him about as vast as that between Tobias Erkner's reality and that of a Nigerian emigrant. Faced with this bamboozle, the optimism Kraft has so arduously scraped together collapses like a sliced soufflé and, putting Erkner's goodwill and the prize money on the line, he draws breath for a rejoinder, a harsh one, formulated with the rigor of a sound European awareness of history and the instinct for realism that comes from such grounding. He will employ the range of his sharply honed instruments: caustic humor, sarcasm, and irony. His rejoinder will be scornful, sardonic, incisive. He wants to shame, destroy, and unmask the two men, this ludicrous would-be pirate in his rank wrestling singlet and this fishy millionaire with his half-baked, childish dreams. Unfortunately, however, the latter has already called for the check without Kraft noticing and just when Kraft is about to let loose, his lips already set in a superior grin of anticipation, a grin with which he intends to underline the bon mot, inspired by Heidegger, about the autonomous laws of technology, which he just thought up as an opening to his ad hoc tirade, when the noodle gratin chef himself comes over to the table in his grease-stained leather apron and announces, after receiving their many-voiced compliments about his ultimate macaroni and cheese, to which the blindsided Kraft also lends his voice, that the gentlemen's dinner is, of course, on the house, because he very much hopes, he says, turning to Erkner and Danneskjöld, that it will serve as his recommendation for a branch on the high seas; after all, nothing is more important for a new community than a common soul and in that light his ultimate *soul cuisine* is predestined, you could say, for the nourishment of the settlers, and furthermore, outside of territorial waters and freed from the endless chicanery he is subjected to every day on the part of the unions and the authorities, he will finally be in a position to significantly increase his profit margin on each panful of noodles sold, and for that he is willing to pay a considerable amount in rent. Erkner and Danneskjöld are thrilled with the idea of pushing back the *frontier* with him and promise to think of him when they put to sea and so he will be hearing from them very soon.

Exactly eighteen minutes after they entered the restaurant, they are back outside on Valencia Street, and a black car with a glowing pink mustache on the dashboard pulls up to the curb. Kraft is hustled into the back seat, followed by Ivan; then Ragnar and the young Eddie, he who had so devotedly waited in line for them then remained silent for the entire meal, say goodbye through the open window. Erkner gets in the front passenger seat and gives the order to leave. Kraft, who always wants to know where he is and can't stand being driven, stares out the window, trying in vain to orient himself. He soon gives up. Tonight, he is prepared to admit, he will have to abandon the reins. He can count his blessings that he wasn't left behind. Kraft turns to his friend, who said little during the meal, in desperate need of agreement, hoping for some sign of understanding, a wink of his good eye, a faint ironic smile, some small gesture that would signal to him, Kraft, that he is not alone in this strange performance and that later, on the drive home, they'll have a good laugh over it. But Ivan has closed his eyes and is massaging the base of his thumb. He looks exhausted. Kraft slumps in his seat and gingerly probes his burned soft palate with the tip of his tongue. The car glides through the city, up and down its steep streets.

ten

History is an arena only one can leave as a victor.

—FORD SAKAGUCHI

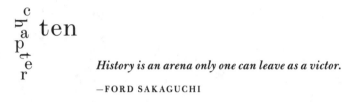

raft held the leather briefcase with the two remaining bottles of Tokay protectively to his chest, while an already downed bottle of wine and a Hungarian paprika salami waged a pitched battle for supremacy in his gullet. There was pushing and shoving on all sides and the gleaming caps of his Italian shoes kept getting stepped on as the glass of broken beer bottles crunched under his shoes' thin leather soles. The crowd, thick on both sides of the Brandenburg Gate, surged down the Unter den Linden boulevard and onto the Pariser Platz, which just a few weeks before had still been part of the death strip. The crowd squeezed in both directions through the narrow breeches in the Wall, which soldiers of the National People's Army had opened two days before Christmas, and flooded the square in front of the Brandenburg Gate, where it encountered a tide of people coming from the Tiergarten.

Kraft had intended to watch the events on television from the sofa in Grunewaldstraße, where he now lived alone, but Ivan—as he wanted to be called since he had moved to California—had other plans. At the crack of dawn on the final day of that turbulent decade, he had rung Kraft's doorbell, which had also been his until a few years ago, and when Kraft, still half-asleep, opened the door, he stormed into the narrow hallway, bringing the musty whiff of a Hungarian couchette car, brandishing a plastic bag that revealed the contours of wine bottles and sausages, and shouted that he had escaped a second time, but this time, not without booty.

István had not been home even once in the eight years since the Hungarian student delegation had taken him to the chess championship as their shirt-washer and forgotten him in a dreary hotel room. Eight years during which he wasn't allowed to see his mother or his father or even his little sister, whom he remembered as a mousy sixteen-year-old with a bad complexion. His father, meanwhile, had died, his mother's hair had become thin, and his sister had a baby at her breast when she opened the door for Ivan. His mother embraced her long-lost son and immediately, even as she patted his cheeks and covered his face with dry kisses, whispered in his ear the first in a litany of reproaches that centered for the most part on the fact that he had left without saying goodbye; how could he have left for the West without telling her, as if he couldn't trust his own mother? István—he very quickly realized that was who he would always be in Budapest—could only have countered this reproach by admitting to his mother that he hadn't had any intention of absconding to West Berlin but had simply been forgotten by his teammates like a single, dirty sock hidden under the bedspread, but he worried that an inadvertent flight would be an even worse excuse for an eight-year absence and for missing his father's funeral.

Despite the reproaches and the missing father, it was a lovely and joyous Christmas celebration for his mother, for his sister, for the radiant, chubby-cheeked infant, and for the baby's walrus-mustached progenitor, who had decided to catch up on all the missed brotherly-in-law drinking bouts in those few quiet, snowy days—for all of them, but not for István, no, not for him, because he had the feeling that the wonderful products from the West that were appearing for the first time in the stores of Budapest, on the festive tables in local homes, and under Christmas trees covered with ornaments, making the holiday a particularly joyous one for his family, had something vulgar about them. He watched disapprovingly as his fellow countrymen blissfully carried video recorders, televisions, and stereo sets out of the stores, as they proudly shivered in their new jeans and leather jackets in the Budapest winter, as they had the cheapest trinkets—which they claimed were Western goods, even though most came from Asia—wrapped in ugly gift paper, as entire families pressed their noses against the richly decorated shop windows; yes, he even disapproved of the red envelopes adorned with golden stars that his sister and her husband handed each other when the presents were exchanged, from which they extricated, with feigned surprise and loud exclamations of delight, plane tickets to Paris they had bought in a travel agency three days prior.

Why did he frown upon his countrymen's reveling in consumption and their hunger for travel? They simply didn't go about it the right way. They were doing it wrong. As consumers they lacked West German sober pragmatism, British understatement, and American insouciance. They were barbarians. They debased the holy act of shopping. Consumption, for Ivan Pánczél, was a serious matter. At least, he convinced himself that this was the source of the disapproval and the bad temper that had dogged him since his arrival in Budapest. Complete nonsense, of course. For several months now, his immediate environment had put him in a state of constant irritation, of heightened tension that had set in coincident with the collapse of the Eastern Bloc. Outwardly he hailed this collapse and the fall of the Iron Curtain loudly and triumphantly as the definitive victory of economic liberalism, but inwardly he had begun to suspect it was a Pyrrhic victory, at least for him personally, since his existence until then had fed on the duality of those systems that now appeared to have been overcome.

As soon as he had earned his first deutsche mark by tutoring a dense high school student in Charlottenburg, he became an enthusiastic consumer. Not of luxury goods, because these were beyond his means—and besides, he didn't particularly covet them. Small, inexpensive things did the trick. Buying things, that's what it was all about, entering into the sacred circulatory system of commerce that went beyond the satisfaction of basic needs and thus became an end in itself, essentially a kind of art for art's sake. But his countrymen didn't understand this art at all, he repeated to himself over that Christmas holiday in Budapest. It quite simply spoiled his pleasure to see that those he had once left behind could now also be consumers. Part of the pleasure associated with every purchase had been the knowledge that he was one of the favored ones, one of the chosen, distinct from the brothers and sisters he had left behind the Iron Curtain, but not like all those consumers in the West who had no experience of the shortage economy, who had never needed to escape. In short, he had allotted himself this special status and now he saw it threatened. This new experience of equality—now even his walrus-mustached, Zwack Unicum–drinking dolt of a brother-in-law could afford a trip to Paris—poisoned his desire to shop once and for all, with the result that almost all his purchases still date from the late '80s; he still wears the large glasses with square metal frames he had bought because the elderly Hayek wore that model, he still drives his 1985 Ford Bronco he bought used the day after he arrived in Palo Alto, and if Barbara didn't intervene every once in a while and drag him to Nordstrom, he would still be wearing sports jackets with shoulder pads and rolled-up sleeves.

The collapse of communism was a disaster that touched every part of his life. Not only did he lose his desire to shop, but his aura as dissident refugee lost its power overnight, and professionally it was a complete catastrophe because a foreseeable end to the Cold War drained his discipline of all the erotic attraction from one day to the next and left it, at least in his students' eyes, of historical interest at most. His first year as a hotshot among the defense intellectuals at Stanford University and the most recent new Fellow at the Hoover Institution on War, Revolution, and Peace had just ended and he was, in his early thirties, already at risk of becoming the custodian of his field of research. After only a few semesters he had to stop offering his catchily titled course Victory Is Possible: Controlled Escalation from First to Last Strikes and to give a lecture course called the History of Nuclear Strategy to a much smaller number of students.

The main reason for his irritation and heightened tension, however, was his fear of the Hungarian intellectuals who could take advantage of their newfound freedom of movement and show up in Stanford as visiting scholars at any moment. What if one of them had been a member of the chess team and, at the sight of Ivan, remembered the championship in Berlin and the departure of the blue Ikarus bus at daybreak? Ivan spent the first half of the '90s in a state of constant worry that one of them would appear and destroy his legend. Even today he would still occasionally sit bolt upright in the middle of the night, bathed in cold sweat, woken by a dream in which a pale young man whom Ivan, heart beating wildly, immediately recognizes as János Rákosi, the captain of the Hungarian university chess team from 1980 to 1984, stands up in the middle of his lecture and points an accusing finger at him, Professor Ivan Pánczél, fellow of the Hoover Institution on War, Revolution, and Peace, teaching the history of nuclear deterrence on the authority of his reputation as Hungarian dissident, political refugee, and chess master; then the young man declares in a shrill voice that still rings in Ivan's ears from their complaints about sweat stains under the sleeves of the ivory-colored polyester jerseys, that this man here, passing himself off as Professor Ivan Pánczél, an expert on nuclear strategy, is nothing but an impostor, none other than the shirt-washer István Pánczél, who had been forgotten in a dreary hotel room in Berlin like a dirty, unmatched sock under the bedspread.

Ivan's fear of being exposed was completely unfounded since all involved had quickly suppressed any memory of the shirt-washer Pánczél after having agreed on a lie at the Czechoslovakian highway rest stop, a lie they promptly adopted as gospel truth, albeit always haunted by a stale aftertaste, so they were, therefore, all too happy to forget the whole business, all, that is, but the intelligence officer who, having accompanied the student national chess team as their minder on the trip to Berlin, was held responsible for the shirt-washer Pánczél's escape to the West and, as a result, was sent into the wilderness, that is, transferred to the puszta as a disciplinary measure, where he contracted before long a case of meningitis from a spoiled can of goulash out of the stocks of the National People's Army, an illness that he barely survived and that left him so utterly feeble-minded he couldn't even remember his mother, much less the shirt-washer Pánczél.

I van led the way. He forged a path through the crowd like a wedge and parted the bellowing masses like a combat swimmer. The irritability and strain he had exported from California to Budapest, then brought with him from there to Berlin, did not dissipate under the effect of the Tokay they'd just downed or of his reunion with Kraft, and meanwhile he could no longer remember why, the day before, when reading an article in the *Magyar Nemzet* about the preparations for the upcoming New Year's festivities in Berlin—the first since the fall of the Wall, which the residents of East and West Berlin were preparing to celebrate together—he had the sudden conviction that he had to be there, upon which he packed his things, shoved a couple bottles of wine and a Hungarian salami in a plastic bag, hurriedly kissed his mother on the forehead, and boarded the night train to Berlin as if the state security services were on his tail. And now that he was here, he at least didn't want to miss the David Hasselhoff concert being held next to the Wall.

The noise was frightening. There was singing and shouting. Fireworks shot out of the crowd into the smoke-filled sky and illuminated the quadriga atop the Brandenburg Gate, on which young men were climbing, brandishing bottles, and dancing, drunk with joy, on the edge of the void. The GDR flag had been lowered, the hammer, compass, and garland torn out, and then raised up the flagpole again, with the powerfully symbolic hole, next to the European flag. Ivan, with Kraft cursing and following in his wake, fought his way westward up to the Wall, on which thousands of people were perched, squeezed tightly together above the swaying reunited German *Volk*. Ivan blazed a roughshod trail across the former death strip, strewn with garbage and broken bottles. Once at the foot of the Wall, they let themselves be pulled up by their hands. There they stood, sweating despite the icy frigidity of the New Year's Eve night and looking triumphantly out over the heads of the jubilant crowd. Kraft pulled one of the bottles of Tokay out of his leather satchel and pulled the cork he had already loosened at home out with his teeth. The syrupy wine ran down their throats, sweet and viscous. Every square centimeter of the Wall seemed to be occupied by revelers, but newcomers kept boarding the concrete slabs with the assistance of those standing above them. Kraft and Ivan were constantly being prompted to grab the hands stretched out to them and pull people up. The two of them stood side by side, clinging to each other and to complete strangers. In a din of shouting, a child, a boy about six years old, was held up to them. The boy raised his thin arms, Kraft grabbed his wrists, pulled him energetically up to eye level, and stared into the boy's face: he saw his own gray eyes with honey-colored flecks in the irises, his own curly hair, a mouth that was still childish but already bore a trace of the same skeptical expression on his own narrow lips. Alarmed, Kraft held the child at arm's length and looked pleadingly for help at Ivan, who stood face-to-face with a woman he had just hoisted up. With her broad face and maternal hips, she stood before Ivan, looking into the weeping eye she had once angrily flailed with a gerbera. Ruth Lambsdorff looked from one to the other in panic, tore her child, who was quite obviously Kraft's too, from his arms, held the boy protectively to her buxom chest, and stepped back in alarm from the Hungarian dissident and chess whizz; in doing so she lost her footing and would certainly have fallen backward off the Wall with her son in her arms, if Ivan, of all people, who recognized her at that very instant as the socialist battle-ax whom he had to thank for his loss of vision, had not instinctively reached for her and prevented her fall, while Kraft stood next to him, gaping and idle.

For a moment, time seemed to stand still as if that decade would never end; blood pounded in the ears of all three, the child looked uncomprehendingly from one to the other. A power from the past penetrated this triangle and sought to push their bodies apart, but there was no escape. They were forced to stand next to one another, squeezed tightly together, the boy crushed between them, and then cheering surged up behind these frozen figures, as if hundreds of thousands of people wanted to celebrate their reunion, a synthesizer began to play, and a singer's voice, amplified a thousandfold, drowned out the crowd. One June morning, some twenty years earlier, he'd been born a rich man's son; he'd had everything that money could buy, but as for freedom, he'd had none, he sang in English—which was fortunate, because what the singer was crooning about wasn't exactly the problem the celebrating citizens of the GDR had suffered. Then a thumping beat set in and David Hasselhoff, standing in a crane basket and urging the crowd to clap in rhythm, was lifted over the masses of people. Countless electric lightbulbs flashed on his leather jacket, and his scarf, knit in a pattern of piano keys, glowed against the night's darkness as thousands of voices joined in the refrain's call for the freedom that had been sought for so long.

I've been looking for freedom
Still the search goes on

The little boy threw up his arms, clapped his small hands to the beat, and joined the chorus with his childish falsetto.

This seemed to release the three adults from their torpor. In a gesture of deliverance, they raised their hands to the heavens and sang freedom's praises with the American TV star, but only to themselves, avoiding each other's eyes and staring into the sky blazing with fireworks.

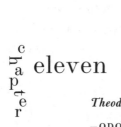

chapter eleven

Theodicy successful, God dead.

—ODO MARQUARD

Jolted awake, Kraft finds himself staring into the gaping beak of a purple finch. He had dreamed he was all alone on a beach in Ceuta facing an enormous machine emitting a laser beam that was sintering an object out of the sand with rapid strokes right in front of the gleaming tips of his shoes, and the object, rising on some invisible mechanism, soon towered above him, revealing layer upon layer of glass, until he found himself looking up at a transparent habitat. The sea surged, waves washed around Kraft's fine shoes. He found refuge on the crystalline island that was floating out to the open sea. Kraft remained completely calm, there was no reason to panic, he knew Gibraltar wasn't far away, and he had everything he needed: a glass bed, a glass toilet, a glass cupboard filled with shimmering glass jars of glass preserves. Suffocating, gurgling cries for help were carried toward him on the wind. Countless ragged figures in wrestling singlets that gleamed like sealskin swam toward his island, stretching their black arms out to his island, clutching at its edges with fingers wrinkled from the salt water, swinging their pinkish soles over the railing. With mute tenacity, Kraft defended his realm, twisted their fingers backward, stepped on cracking phalanges, running from port to starboard and back again, striking, pushing, and kicking, but there were too many of them. Then Herb handed him an oar and Kraft beat at the heads that popped up over the rail in a frenzied dance, one head, one face, one blow, there, another one, wham, bang, and then he slipped, staggered, tumbled, toppled backward over the railing, his fingers slipping on the glass, the water closing over his head—at which point he sat bolt upright and stared into the gaping beak of that purple finch.

He thrashes his legs wildly to free them from the sweat-soaked sheets, heedlessly sets his bare feet on the carpet, and grips the cool bed frame with one hand. Good Lord, Kraft thinks, why on earth was I beating those miserable heads? Why would I do such a thing? That's not who I am at all. And the oar, I barely get my hands on it again, at least on one of the two, before losing it again. He rubs his eyes, his nose, snorts and brushes away the hair stuck to his forehead. That damn Erkner disrupted me completely with his blather.

Erkner had dragged them to a bar, high up in a glass tower

somewhere in the Financial District. Kraft sat by the window and looked down into the street canyons through which fireflies left glowing traces, and then he looked up along the facades to the top of the Transamerica Pyramid, which jutted into the evening sky like a pharaonic tomb. Somewhere down below, in those hills, Johanna sat, spoon in hand, in a small wooden house, perhaps in the glow of a kitchen light she had just turned on. Kraft was hungry. To his own astonishment, he already regretted his mac and cheese, which had been whisked away, barely touched, from under his nose. And an obsequious waitress had just removed the bowl of mixed nuts from the table on Erkner's request that she take it away. In its place, a bottle of locally distilled rye whiskey was brought, from which Erkner poured generous portions before perching on the edge of his petrol-blue midcentury chair, his back very straight, his tumbler balanced on the palm of his hand, holding forth. In an effort to adopt an interested posture, Kraft had imitated him but he soon sank under the weight of his interlocutor's unfailingly contradictory pronouncements and retreated to the safety of the chair cushions. He felt as shattered as he had months before, when he opened the PDF attachment in Ivan's e-mail and looked at the boyish face with cold eyes that was now directly in front of him, so close he could have touched the flat nose with his fingertips if he'd only had the strength to stretch out his arm.

Erkner seemed to be possessed by an urgent need to deliver an exhaustive explanation of his worldview in articulate sentences of flawless clarity that sounded alternately like slogans and professions of faith, statements he launched with great emphasis but without any visible emotion over the kidney-shaped table that stood between them.

He feels closer to Catholicism with its theological complexity and intellectual rigor, Erkner had said, than to the arbitrariness of Protestantism. He is a devout Christian, he declared, his gaze fixed just past

Kraft's left ear. *Christianity is true.* And because there was no division in Erkner's intellectual makeup between his convictions, which Kraft felt belonged primarily to the private sphere, and his guiding principles as an entrepreneur, in the same way as the most diverse subjects merged into each other seamlessly and organically in Erkner's disquisitions and obscured the precarious structure of his arguments, Kraft was overcome by a diffuse malaise that he initially attributed to strong drink on a stomach empty of anything that could absorb it. But then Erkner explained after just a few sentences—a few sentences with which, nonetheless, he appeared to have covered enormous ground without Kraft noticing how he had advanced his argument—that he had always loathed the authorities because they reined in the originality of thought with the bridle of the past and actual present and so impeded rapid progress toward prospective futures and curbed reflection on the present future, and in so doing also limited the range of possibilities for the future to come. One's approach to the world, he continued, should be as independent as possible from existing interpretations and those imposed by the authorities, in order to avoid well-trodden paths, which is absolutely essential for all thought and action in the technology sector, since only the new will guarantee a better future for humankind. Intellectual independence is the sole guarantor for freedom. It took Kraft a long time to ascribe his malaise to the utter irreconcilability of the particular elements in Erkner's discourse. It was as if he were being served a liverwurst milkshake, but one prepared so skillfully and delivered with such assurance that the evident incompatibility of the ingredients only became noticeable when they lost their artful form in his stomach and began to rebel against each other. How the devil, he wondered, can a profession of Catholic faith be reconciled with a rejection of all authority? Before Kraft could formulate an objection, he was subjected to a new sleight of hand, whitewashed with the utterly inconceivable—immortality—presented with the same matter-of-factness with which one would treat a technical problem that could soon be resolved with a spot of financing and ingenuity. Human mortality was a problem of great, perhaps even utmost, urgency and that was why he was investing a not inconsiderable sum in overcoming it by funding a biogerontologist's institute. Defeating death is entirely within the realm of the possible; death is, after all, nothing but a disease not substantially different from the flu or stomach cancer; probably not in his lifetime, but you have to think of the future. One thing he doesn't understand, mind you, is how so many people willingly capitulate to death. Our society is convinced that death is unpredictable and unavoidable.

Kraft didn't see how Erkner's desire for immortality could coexist with his profession of Christian faith whether in a Protestant or a Catholic context. However, to his surprise and deep discouragement, he lacked confidence in his counterarguments, obvious as they were. It was inconceivable, he thought, that such a successful man would put millions into a project that wasn't thoroughly thought out. Erkner, in the meantime, had left death far behind and embarked on what was obviously his favorite subject, the future, or the futures, to be more precise, since there seemed to be a wide array of forms possible, of which only one was desirable. Luckily that one could be completely planned out. He was even able to draw a small diagram of it on his cocktail napkin with practiced strokes of his Montblanc fountain pen and he impressed Kraft by effortlessly writing the script upside down so that it was legible for the person sitting across from him. The planet, he explained with the aid of his sketch, has been in a state of crisis for some time because mankind has lost its faith in a quantifiable world, a quantifiable future. In the golden years of the 1950s and the decades that followed, mankind had been guided by a concrete optimism that had its source in the United States and the technological and scientific progress being made here, that is, the belief that the future would be better than the present if we did what was necessary and worked hard at it. There was general agreement on what that better future should look like. But today mankind is in the grip of a universal pessimism. An abstract pessimism is making minds dull, especially in Europe. People are convinced the future will necessarily be bleak and don't have the slightest idea what to do about it. All that's left for Europeans is to wait for the inevitable decline and enjoy life without bothering to act; and that's precisely the reason for Europeans' leisure mentality. In America, by contrast, a phase of abstract optimism began in the early '80s and is most clearly visible in the growth of the financial sector, the sole purpose of which is to amass money, without, however, any idea of how to create a better future.

Kraft was now completely confused since after he'd received the invitation to Stanford he naturally had studied Erkner's Wikipedia page, where he learned that Erkner had worked for a considerable time in the financial sector and had bet against currencies and energy prices using his own funds and had landed in a precarious state during the financial crisis. At a loss, Kraft looked at Ivan, but the latter seemed to be avoiding eye contact. Apparently indifferent, he just sat next to Erkner and watched the ice cubes in his glass melt. In these dire times of abstract optimism, Erkner continued, lawyers and bankers are the leaders. That said, an inclination toward concrete optimism and the belief in a future that can actually be planned for are essential, and at the end of this cultural revolution in which mankind will shake off the yoke of chance, engineers will once again be the spearhead of mankind. With these words, a flash of enthusiasm sailed past Kraft's right ear for the first time.

Hah, chance, Kraft thinks, that's one thing this Erkner doesn't like. He stands up and starts to pace back and forth across McKenzie's room in his underwear. Naturally he doesn't like it, because chance is at odds with his elitism. Life is not a game of chance, Erkner had declared and quoted a few authorities in support of his convictions. Shallow men believe in luck or in circumstance. That strong men believe in cause and effect is something Emerson knew. And Amundsen believed that success awaited those who had put their affairs in order. Others call it luck . . . But a tweet by Twitter co-founder Jack Dorsey was also quoted as proof: "success is never accidental . . ."

Erkner wasn't content to invoke only these authorities, but—before Kraft could counter with Jonathan Swift's comment that the "power of fortune is confessed only by the miserable; for the happy impute all their success to prudence or merit"—he made sure to bring in the Pareto principle or, broadly speaking, the power law, according to which, inequality in the distribution of wealth is an unavoidable worldwide phenomenon: yes, it's abundantly clear that our world is governed by power law in both its natural and social dimensions; for example, Pareto had already been able to show that land ownership in Italy followed the classic 80/20 rule, that is, 80 percent of the land is owned by 20 percent of the population, which was demonstrated just as naturally as the fact that 80 percent of the peas in Vilfredo Pareto's garden were produced by 20 percent of the pea pods. From this Erkner easily deduced that among men too there is a mere handful of productive individuals and geniuses whose actions bring about progress for all mankind. Thus by recognizing the Pareto principle as a governing law of the universe, we can establish that economic disparity is a law of nature.

Kraft interrupts his pacing in front of the posters of basketball players, which set him thinking. Although he is blessed with a slightly taller than average height, these giants would tower head and shoulders over him. Nature grants only very few the stature of a basketball player, but not everyone who is six feet eight can play basketball well. No, that takes hard work. On the other hand, there are talented basketball players of average height, and anyway it's not a good example because height is not determined by exponential distribution, as Kraft knows. But does this speak for or against Erkner's argument?

Ah, once again our Kraft hears the faint call over the battlements: *It's not that simple, nothing ever is . . .* But why does he hear the call right now, at this very moment? Why does his laboriously constructed intellectual fortress reveal its vulnerability in Erkner's presence? Well, we already have our suspicions as to the answer: various elements of Erkner's thought and personality are not entirely foreign. Despite all their apparent differences, Kraft and Erkner have more in common than Kraft is comfortable admitting and we can assume that Kraft's antipathy is fed to a significant extent precisely by this fact. Kraft has never yet met anyone in whom the natures of the hedgehog and the fox are in such open conflict. As he sat across from Erkner in the bar and had to listen meekly to his harangue, it seemed obvious to him that Erkner was essentially vulpine, but suffered, at the same time, from such longing for clarity and unambiguity that he found refuge in erinaceidaeness, which must have been a great torment for the man, since it isn't possible for a fox to be a hedgehog, as Kraft was well aware. As a result he stretched and extended himself back into his fox shape, which he also hardly seemed able to bear. Erkner was like a fox chasing its own tail, spinning faster and faster like a dervish until his nimble body—which was able to trot at such a fleet-footed, springy pace that it even seemed capable of running over water— began to get denser and denser, whirling in an ever faster pirouette until it whirred itself into a hedgehog, but still the spinning didn't stop and the hedgehog rolled itself into such a tight ball that its quills pierced its own soft underbelly and it flinched, stretched, and extended itself in all directions, flinging its limbs outward and so turning back into a fox chasing its own tail . . . It's no wonder someone like that is so profoundly disoriented that he doesn't realize he's lost his bearings and even the most blatant contradictions strike him as compatible. Over time, such oscillation must wear down one's soul. Kraft almost feels sorry for him and this, for Kraft, is certainly a rare sensation. He would have liked for Erkner to have an István of his own, someone who could have opened Erkner's eyes to the porcupine option, but for that Kraft is sure it's too late. Erkner is too old and presumably also too wealthy.

Lord knows, Kraft is no stranger to the cult of genius . . . But let's not go overboard . . . And this return to the so-called laws of nature, which, however, are only valid when they're useful . . . And that unpleasantly unapologetic elitism . . . But hang on! Isn't there something to be squeezed out of this? Isn't there something on this in Pope? Kraft turns on the desk lamp and searches excitedly through his stacks of books for Pope's *Essay on Man*. In the third epistle, maybe? No, the fourth. Kraft doesn't actually need to look it up, thanks to his phenomenal memory, it's been buzzing in his head for some time, but he wants to see it in black-and-white. Let's see . . . Here it is:

Order is Heav'n's first law; and this confest,
Some are, and must be, greater than the rest,
More rich, more wise . . .

Suddenly he knows what he has to do. He sets his alarm for seven, smooths out the rumpled sheets, spreads the patchwork quilt over them, turns out the light, and crawls into bed. For a brief moment, he is torn between euphoric drive for action and boundless relief, but the latter soon wins the upper hand and releases Kraft into slumber.

nowing what he has to do. What a sweet sensation for our Kraft. It's a fleeting sensation, Kraft knows, and that's precisely why he has to seize the moment, for all too often doubts soon return and steadily gnaw away at one's strength.

Did he know what he had to do when, after the cheering for David Hasselhoff had died away, Ruth Lambsdorff laid her hands on her son's shoulders, turned him to face Kraft, and introduced him by saying that this was Daniel, whom she had named after Cohn-Bendit?

Ivan's lips trembled. Dumbfounded, he looked from the boy's face to his friend's and back again, swept his good eye over Ruth's ample bosom and up to her broad features, pointed an accusing finger at her, followed by an American swear word, then leaped off the wall and fled east. Kraft did not hold him back. Instead, he jumped down on the other side of the wall, pushed his way through the jubilant crowd without looking back and disappeared into the gloom of the Tiergarten.

It took Kraft six days—one day for each year of his son's life—to forgive Ruth for not telling him that he was a father and three additional days for him to forgive her for naming their son after Cohn-Bendit. Then he set out in search of her. No one in the Diener remembered the woman he described to the staff and the guests as not a classical beauty but a striking personality, as with awkward gestures he tried to convey what it was he found so striking about her. No, no one knew of any such woman in the Diener, nor, therefore, of the young boy who might occasionally have been with her, whom Kraft also mentioned; a young boy who was his spitting image.

He had more luck at the School of Fine Arts. In a studio with grimy windows, where the plaster dust dirtied his freshly polished shoes, they remembered Ruth Lambsdorff very well. She had worked as Günther Ackerknecht's assistant until just a few months ago but then the two of them had an argument and he'd fired her, a young man whose skin, hair, and coveralls were coated with a dusting of white powder that looked like mold, confided in a whisper. No, unfortunately he didn't have Lambsdorff's home address, but surely the professor could help, he added, his thin face contorted into a malicious grin, his expression just like the one on the gaunt face of the plaster figure he'd been scratching at with a rusty nail.

Kraft found Ackerknecht sitting outdoors behind the studio building. Despite the cold he wore only a vest of coarse corduroy over his carpenter's pants and he didn't appreciate being disturbed while smoking. The professor sullenly scraped his boots in the mud and rubbed a hand over the sparse gray bristles on his massive skull, crowning his head with cigarette ash. Kraft clutched his briefcase to his chest. This was exactly the kind of man who intimidated him: beefy, pink, crude. He tentatively made his request: he had been told that the professor might know Mrs. Lambsdorff's home address. Ackerknecht coughed. Yes, absolutely, he knew the address. Then he coughed again and said nothing. Might it be possible to get it from him? Kraft was subjected to a perusal that seeped through his short wool coat like the winter chill. He didn't seem stupid enough to be the police and wasn't unfriendly enough either, for that matter—was he a debt collector? No, no, Kraft hastened to reassure the professor, his acquaintance with Mrs. Lambsdorff was of a strictly personal nature. Ackerknecht tilted his head to the side and scrutinized him further with narrowed eyes, then tapped his temple with two fingers clamped on a self-rolled cigarette. You're little Danny's father, aren't you? he asked. Yes, as a matter of fact, he did have reason to think so. Think so? Ackerknecht snorted, Breker himself couldn't have created a better likeness of you two. He didn't think it would be right to divulge Ms. Lambsdorff's address. Ackerknecht dropped his cigarette and ground it roughly into the dirt. And yet that was exactly why he was happy to do it. With a chewed-up pencil stub he first licked, he wrote the address on a slip of paper Kraft hurriedly pulled from his briefcase. As he handed Kraft the paper he said, Don't forget to tell her that you got her address from me. Good luck. He coughed and walked off with a tired wave of his meaty paw.

Ruth was, in fact, anything but delighted when Kraft showed up outside her door in Kreuzberg; nevertheless, she invited him into her small apartment that smelled of coal heating. Kraft took from his briefcase the Ninja Turtle action figure he had bought on the way and, under Ruth's disapproving gaze, he held it out to his son, who clung tightly to the doorframe of his room. The boy took the stranger's unfamiliar present without a word and disappeared into his bedroom. Ruth asked Kraft into the kitchen, put the kettle on, and listened silently to his reproaches as she waited for the water to boil. She didn't try to defend herself, since she had wondered over the years whether it was right to deprive the boy of his father and even sometimes if it was wrong to keep Kraft's son a secret from him, but that was rare, since she hardly ever thought of Kraft at all. In any event, she wasn't one to apologize.

Ruth sat down across from Kraft and blew on her tea. She felt tired. Exhausted, somehow. If Kraft had shown up a few months earlier, she probably wouldn't have let him over the threshold. But right then she didn't have the energy to stop him. As it was with Ivan, although for very different reasons, the turn taken by German history was not to her advantage. She'd already sensed that her Berlin and her

West Berlin life were doomed, and even though she certainly wasn't uncritical of the Eastern Bloc regimes, she was sorry that history was rushing toward this inevitable end. She knew that living in this enclave was like living in a bubble and that the way of life she'd chosen could only be realized here because the necessary attitude could only be preserved in these unique historical circumstances. Ruth was, accordingly, profoundly torn. The collapse of the Eastern Bloc, and German reunification, which seemed ever more likely, threatened her niche, yet at the same time, she was ashamed of this small-minded egoism because she thought she ought to be happy for the millions who would, as it were, become free. Still, she intuited that the breakdown of socialism would result in a reduction of alternatives, and could see that this reduction would only encourage those forces intending to impose an interpretation of freedom different from hers.

And then there was her falling-out with Ackerknecht. Ackerknecht, who had encouraged her when she was still a student and had offered her a position as his assistant—for which she had been duly grateful—after she received her degree. Soon she was more than just his assistant because Ackerknecht was just another windbag, albeit of a somewhat more taciturn sort. He beleaguered Ruth and everyone around him with his inexhaustible creative drive. Laconic and uncommunicative verbally, he released an endless stream of larger-than-life sculptures from his studio into the world. Untold depictions of his daughter who had died in an automobile accident, which he angrily hacked from marble, cut from rusty car bodies with a welding torch, or roughly hewed from the trunks of oak trees with a chain saw. On good days he created mawkish sculptures of girls, on bad days he devoted himself to creating mangled bodies of children, and when he was drinking, he fashioned both with stylized angel wings. Even in his most depressed phases, during which he became completely mute and didn't say a word for days on end, his creative drive didn't flag. At a table in his studio, he wordlessly filled casts of his scrotum—creating these molds from plaster dressing was one of Ruth's duties as assistant—with miniature filigree scenes in silver thread, from his dreams, which was his way of processing the testicular cancer he had developed shortly after his daughter's death. After the operation he'd had his empty scrotal sac filled with two marble balls he'd polished himself, and their soft clicking had a wonderfully soothing effect on Ruth when, her head resting on Ackerknecht's meaty thigh, she gently weighed the now useless organ in the hollow of her hand.

It was thus Ackerknecht's manic productivity that triggered Ruth's well-known weakness and unfortunately also crippled her own creative energy, even though, to his credit, Ackerknecht tried to support and encourage her work as best he could in his dour way, which was the only way he had. Ackerknecht's volubility in clay and plaster, in marble and silver thread, in sheet metal and oak, mowed her down and left her feeling utterly wrung out and incapable of action.

She would never have gotten away if she hadn't realized one morning that she couldn't possibly impose life with Ackerknecht on Danny any longer—or rather life with Ackerknecht's dead daughter, versions of whom streamed out of the studio in various degrees of infirmity and in numbers fit to fill a regiment—because her son was becoming increasingly withdrawn and anemic, for which latter ailment the doctors could find no cause.

With his second cup of tea, Kraft left the past behind and turned without ado to the future, in which he saw himself playing an important role in his son's life, a role to which he was clearly entitled and which he intended to take up immediately. With these words he stood up and, ignoring Ruth's weak protestations, strode into his son's room to join again what nature had never intended, he supposed, to be sundered. He had often pictured this reunion over the previous days with the hope that it would prove a moment of sublimity with the cathartic power to transform fear and dread into pity and return things in his life to a state of beauty.

The moment didn't turn out to be quite as sublime as he'd imagined it, because kneeling before the child, he was overtaken by stammering embarrassment, which was reflected in Danny's face as fear and dread and in the end it was the sheer wretchedness of the scene that woke a feeling of pity in Ruth and this prompted her to leave her monitoring post in the doorway and enter the room. She took her son's hand, sat next to him on the edge of the bed, and explained in a straightforward way that this was his father, whom she'd mentioned now and again, back in Berlin from his long trip far away, and now, if it was all right with Danny, he'd like to do things with him once in a while. The child nodded mutely and kneaded the face of the green rubber reptile.

Kraft kept his word and, over Ruth's weakening resistance, intruded into their lives and came to collect both of them at least twice a week for a joint outing. Unfortunately for him, with regard to the shape of family life, he had many abstract ideals but very little practical imagination, so that the visits to the zoo, to museums and ice cream parlors, were becoming repetitive and he was forced to leave the planning of their afternoons together to Ruth. Deep down, he was grateful and, freed from this burden, he was able to fully recognize and appreciate the natural maternal quality that had made such a deep impression on him at their first meeting.

Things took their expected course in this historical-biographical constellation. Ruth's intrinsic weakness developed in sync with what one could call Kraft's "good run." There were hardly any academic conferences willing to do without a lecture by this dynamic young thinker, whose stupendous learning, elegant rhetoric, and bold propositions captivated his audiences and whose essays filled the best specialist journals at a frightening tempo. His name was mentioned whenever there was an important chair to fill in Germany. Kraft managed to give everyone the impression that he was the man of the hour, that he was one of the few thinkers around with an intellect able to grasp and comment upon the age adequately. The invitation to fill the chair in rhetoric at the University of Tübingen and follow in the footsteps of the great Walter Jens resurrected in Kraft the utterly bourgeois dreams of family life he had buried years before when he sat next to István on the sofa on Grunewaldstraße. He blathered on about them to Ruth until she yielded to him out of sheer exhaustion and was soon pregnant for the second time.

Kraft dragged the defenseless woman to the registry office and made a Lambsdorff into a Kraft—incidentally, the only thing he occasionally reproached himself for in later years. He traveled to Tübingen without Ruth, who suffered from chronic placental insufficiency, a condition which surprised him in light of her broad hips, and there he bought an apartment near the banks of the Neckar River, on the top floor of a sixteenth-century house—such a perfect and gratifying stage set for his familial dreams that he went heavily into debt to acquire it. His future home office had a view of the Tübinger Stift, the Evangelical seminary, and if he leaned out the window a bit and craned his neck, he could see the top of the Hölderlin Tower. His newly acquired property included a spacious garret with beams of fir from the Black Forest. Kraft promised his wife he would turn it into an atelier for her to take up her artistic work again.

Kraft's small family moved to Tübingen before the birth of their second child. The parquet floors gleamed, the autumn sunlight shone through the finely mullioned windows, the sandstone floor in the vestibule, crossed by thousands of steps, promised them a part in history. After lengthy negotiations with the monument-protection authority, craftsmen had brought natural light into the garret by installing two large skylights. Kraft promised to take care of the insulation and the interior construction himself, very soon.

Ruth packed up her apartment in Kreuzberg without resistance and, with a feeling of relief that surprised her, she turned her back on Berlin, which was busy preparing for the reunification celebration, to bear a second child of Kraft's with the difference that this time, following his idea of a modern bourgeois marriage, he devotedly took care of her whenever his new position as full professor allowed.

Did he do the right thing? Maybe so, but probably for the wrong reasons. Who can say for certain? Things weren't that simple.

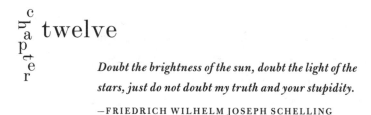

chapter

twelve

Doubt the brightness of the sun, doubt the light of the stars, just do not doubt my truth and your stupidity.

—FRIEDRICH WILHELM JOSEPH SCHELLING

fat chance Kraft knows what he has to do. Doubts come faster than he's able to marshal the previous night's euphoria into a consistent train of thought. Failing euphoria, he struggles instead to grasp the thread through pragmatism and systematic thought, because, if he remembers correctly, that was precisely the source of the energy that had filled him in McKenzie's room. I must obtain freedom for me, for Heike, and for the twins, Kraft tells himself. For that, I need to bring home one million dollars. In order to bring that million home, I have to answer that blasted essay question and do it better than everyone else. But what does "better" mean in this context? To Erkner's greater satisfaction, since he has the last word.

Here Kraft hesitates, because in the light of day, his train of thought lacks the profundity night had lent it and is revealed in all its unspeakable ugliness: vulgar, common, and functionalist. It can't possibly be that simple, can it? Simplicity born of opportunism, have I come to this? Kraft has to ask himself, and Rumsfeld seems to be smiling at him less scornfully than usual. Maybe, with a bit of goodwill, you could even call the smile encouraging. And isn't that a trace of compassion in the former secretary of defense's features? Has it come to this? Yes, indeed, it has.

Kraft pulls himself together, tears the scribbled pages from the pad, and writes in capital letters on a fresh sheet of paper: THEODICY AND TECHNODICY: OPTIMISM FOR A YOUNG MILLENNIUM. WHY WHATEVER IS, IS RIGHT AND WHY WE CAN STILL IMPROVE IT. And underneath: *What would Erkner answer?* He circles the latter question several times with his fountain pen and, after some thought, at a loss, he adds an exclamation point.

For God's sake, he can do this!

Assuming for a moment that this is the best of all worlds, then evil must necessarily be part of it. Erkner's God . . . Or is it Erkner himself? No, first God, then Erkner . . . He'll get around to flattering Erkner's cult of genius later. Erkner's God, therefore, has realized the world not as good liberated from evil, but as the best of all possible worlds in which evil still and necessarily exists. Kraft can get this much from Leibniz. Absolute perfection is an attribute only of God

Himself; in the realm of creation, however, it is for that very reason an impossibility.

That's really very good, for a beginning . . . Of course, some of his colleagues will find him ridiculous, but at least he's setting out his line of reasoning for Erkner's satisfaction on a religious foundation right from the start. And he can iron things out later when he brings it all back to the ground of reality. Erkner doesn't seem to have any problem with contradictions.

Come on . . . Keep going . . .

Evil—it is thus necessary . . . and it IS . . . of this there is no doubt. Now it's a matter of pointing out why evil isn't so bad. Maybe he should move straight to *the Great Chain of Being* . . . Chain is good, it sounds so mechanical, so neatly structured and tangible: link by link, one after the other, you can pull yourself backward until *the spade of knowledge* buckles on hitting the bedrock of the ultimate truth.

Kraft gazes pensively at the fluorescent light and indulges in a brief daydream about that ultimate truth, which appears in his mind's eye as a silvery boulder, massive, heavy, harder than any other substance, of a flawless splendor and with a surface as smooth as glass, so sheer that not a single particle of dust sticks to it. An object in whose existence he can only believe in rare moments, but what moments they are, moments of consummate purity . . .

All right, back to the chain . . . Of course, you can also use such a chain to drag yourself forward, you can follow it link by link into a future that has been forged like the chain. The future, Erkner likes that.

The Great Chain of Being. Here Kraft can elegantly turn to Pope, originator of the phrase they are meant to prove correct: *Whatever is, is right.* Mankind's ability—no he'd better talk about value rather than ability, so that the monetary aspect resonates from the beginning; he can close the circle later—so, mankind's intrinsic value, but also the value of the individual, is commensurate with his position in the All, in the Great Chain of Being. And, as Pope writes, man is at a middle state between god and beast. And this in-between state is the source of his inner strife. Strife, that's good, it will speak directly to Erkner's subconscious. On the other hand . . . man as a deficient being? Erkner would certainly have trouble recognizing himself as such. Maybe better to leave that out. Kraft writes *poss. leave out* in the margin and adds an exclamation point. Then he crosses out the exclamation point. What is it with all these exclamation points, which he otherwise avoids? Avoids on principle!

But he needs these weaknesses and deficiencies to pursue his argument. Naturally, mankind's position is not determined solely by his weaknesses, but also by his strengths. Maybe he should just emphasize the strengths more. Kraft writes *emphasize strengths* in the margin and adds a question mark. That's tricky, though, it's precisely the individual's weaknesses that guarantees the cohesion of the chain since they must be compensated for by the strengths of others. But, and here Kraft finds the solution for his minor difficulty, it's exactly through this mechanism that weaknesses become for Pope *happy frailties* that function as a kind of cement for the entire marvelous construct. Weaknesses may well be a great evil for the individual, but they are, so to speak, a necessary condition for the good of the whole. And somehow, this is, indeed, true, or so Kraft tries to convince himself. The suffering of an individual is nothing next to the greatness of the whole. This—Kraft is suddenly struck by the flawless logic—is indisputable, because, after all, it's not for nothing that the statement says *Whatever is, is right.*

But isn't that rather unjust? someone objects from the audience.

(Kraft likes to picture an audience when he's thinking.) Certainly not, Kraft retorts to the impertinent simpleton, because this is merely a question of distributive justice, and:

(a) Pope has already established that "some are, and must be, greater than the rest, More rich, more wise . . ."

And furthermore:

(b) we can have complete confidence in the trickle-down effect. The more the ones on top possess, the more will trickle down to those below . . . more of everything: money, intelligence, education, etc. This is, to some extent, a well-known law of nature . . . A chain, even . . . and obviously it should not be thought of as horizontal, but as vertical, like those chains that hang from the roof gutter into a rain barrel, just as it should be thought of simultaneously as diachronic and synchronic—this last remark has nothing to do with the matter at hand but works wonderfully well as an *argumentum cerei nebulosi.*

Tying together the trickle-down effect and the Great Chain of Being, why hadn't he thought of this before? Now he was coming into his own. It would be easier going from here. Now he could simply bludgeon his audience with the timbers of neoclassical theory and market liberalism. Supply-side economics, laissez-faire, the invisible hand, self-regulating market forces, individualism, utilitarianism, personal responsibility, et cetera and so on. And the best part will be that no one expects this from a professor of rhetoric. He just has to be sure he takes up a cudgel for the monopolies Erkner praised so enthusiastically in the bar and that somewhere he adds that competition is for losers. He doesn't have to worry about inconsistencies. Maybe he can even justify inconsistency, somehow. Maybe he'll just say that coherent reasoning is self-evidently indispensable, but contradiction is an element of reasoning, too, as this sentence itself proves. He'll have to put it more elegantly, of course. *State more elegantly*, he writes in the margin, *fecundity of contradictory modes . . . /poss. Eristic Dialectic* → *Schopenhauer / Topics / or something in this vein.*

And then, then he can also bring in Vogl and his concept of oikodicy. Just as theodicy advances the idea that it's possible to justify God's goodness despite the obvious presence of evil in the world, Vogl proposes, in analogy, that oikodicy advances the idea that the justness of capitalism can be defended, despite the obvious presence of evil in the world, as, so to speak, an economy of salvation, if one embraced it as a law of nature, with a quasi-religious conviction. Poverty, hunger, injustice are all, as it were, of inherent necessity to the system in service of the whole. The system organizes the social order, which then becomes tantamount to a natural law, and because it's all so wonderfully systematic, everything can be calculated and predicted, ergo . . . the future can be planned. Kraft can almost see how Erkner's gaze during his lecture would finally, after a lifetime of wandering, come to rest and hang on his, Kraft's, lips.

Vogl, to be sure, meant it all critically and presented the replacement of theodicy, that is the justification of God, with oikodicy, the quasi-religious justification of capitalism, as one of the great problems of our time, but where Vogl speaks of phantasms and denounces the religious, imaginary, and spectral aspects of economic events, Kraft can speak systematically of their visionary aspects. This will all point wonderfully to a still better future and reframe Vogl's sotto voce Berlin pessimism as a concrete optimism to Erkner's taste. If Vogl catches wind of this, he will never say another word to Kraft, but Kraft is quite willing to accept this as a pleasant side effect.

So, now he just absolutely has to work in technology and technodicy as the essay requires. Technodicy seeks to justify the existence of technology in the face of the evil in the world. A bit difficult, Kraft fears; after all, in this case, it isn't God sitting in the dock, or some economic system that's been dressed up with an aura of divine ordainment; no, it's mankind in person. Sure, you can claim, along with some cultural critics and technological pessimists, that technology isn't actually a human invention, but something already extant in the realm of ideas, ready-made, as it were, and, subject to a dynamic of its own, developing autonomously, with mankind merely its slave, panting in pursuit . . . But surely this isn't what Erkner wants to hear. No, Kraft has to present technology as mankind's means of self-empowerment: the brilliant, inventive engineer—and his equally brilliant and daring financial backer—who will create a better world with the help of technology. And the evils that are brought into the world by technology, well, Kraft will have to declare them necessary for the purpose and the good of the whole.

And what about the bomb? The great sin of Hiroshima? The same presumptuous voice from the audience interrupts Kraft's lecture again: Do you consider that a necessary evil, too?

Ah, the bomb, Kraft replies with glee. Thank you for your question because, you see, that's a perfect illustration of how things are never so simple, since, considered in the right light, there is no sin of Hiroshima. It's Ivan's light that he imagines he's shining into this dark corner, the same brilliant beam of light Ivan had shone into the world in a whole series of scientific works. The so-called sin of Hiroshima, he'll be able to reason, along with Ivan, is nothing more than an empty phrase, given that recent computer simulations of the subject unequivocally show that the invention of the atomic bomb and the demonstration of its destructive power in Hiroshima prevented a third world war. Only the threat of an atomic holocaust kept the Cold War from escalating into a hot one, since neither of the two blocs was willing to pay the price of total nuclear annihilation. Just imagine that the atomic bomb had never been invented. Say nuclear fission, whether controlled or uncontrolled, was impossible. What then? The answer is obvious and is confirmed by all the computer modeling. Absent the threat of nuclear escalation, there would unquestionably have been a war with conventional weapons between the blocs: a third world war, with machine guns, tanks, bombs, fighter planes, and other such armaments, but far more devastating than the Second World War due to the more highly advanced non-nuclear weapons technology developed between 1978 and 1982, the period during which the predictive model (Pánczél, et al.)—an extremely complex model, as it had to take the influence of nuclear technology on history out of the equation—considered the probability of conventional war to be greatest. Yes, armaments between '78 and '82 had become significantly more effective than those utilized between the years '39 and '45, so you had to calculate the number of victims in such a hypothetical war to be around seven hundred million (+/-8 percent). Ergo, the invention of the atomic bomb has, summa summarum, if you subtract the conservatively estimated one hundred thirty thousand dead in Hiroshima (he's not sure at the moment how to justify the dead in Nagasaki, he'll have to ask Ivan that tonight), saved six hundred million eight hundred seventy thousand lives. It was for the greater good, so to speak. Once again: what the individual experiences as evil proves to be a necessity for the whole and can therefore be justified.

So much for the sin of Hiroshima. Kraft sees the troublemaker in his mental audience buckle under the force of his reasoning and sink into embarrassed thought.

The best thing would be to present technology as a synthesis of faith and capitalism because it most clearly manifests mankind's divinely ordained self-empowerment—the use of mankind's God-given freedom, freedom . . . right, he's rather neglected freedom. In the margin, Kraft writes *Freedom manifests itself in technology!*

And from here it is but a small step to the ultimate self-empowerment, defeating mortality with technology and making man a god. Everything Erkner said the night before about death as a disease that could be overcome suddenly makes sense to Kraft. He can also no longer see the contradictions he thought he'd found between Erkner's profession of Christian faith and his desire for earthly immortality. Substantiating it theologically would be a piece of cake. Man must become a god sooner or later, otherwise God wouldn't have created man in His image and wouldn't have granted him freedom and the potential for development. And the analogy has an absolutely astonishing beauty: God created man in His image just as man will create robots in *his* image, and at some point (soon, he hoped, Erkner had said) the robot will become man (*or the other way round?* Kraft notes in the margin)—and just as God will welcome man's divine transformation, we humans will welcome the human transformation of technology: the Singularity. These will be the fireworks Kraft will set off to conclude his essay: the Singularity, that moment, so often invoked, when technological progress will accelerate and artificial intelligence will overtake the intelligence of its creator: the melding of man and machine . . . *transhumanism, posthumanism, the transcendence of our species*, Kraft notes, as well as *posthuman transtheotechnism.* A new age will dawn, so new and so different that no one, not even a visionary of Erkner's caliber, can as yet describe it. But one thing Kraft can promise, it will be good . . . so good!

It has to be!

Kraft has thought himself into a state of ecstasy. Beads of sweat pearl on his brow. His writing hand has cramped up. He's been writing faster and faster, leaving behind his pen an increasingly illegible trace of his exuberant enthusiasm. Is it possible that in just three hours he has succeeded in doing what he failed to do day after day for weeks?

Kraft leafs back to the first page, where he wrote the essay question out in capital letters in the top margin, and begins reading his work. He makes a few notes here and there, adds a sentence or two, crosses some out. But before long he sets down his pen, wipes his forehead with his shirtsleeve, and then about halfway through gives up entirely . . . what a load of pretentious bullshit.

There is absolutely no way he'll deliver anything like this. He's not that desperate. And then his new iPhone buzzes on the table and the panic that grips him when he sees Heike's number on the screen and declines the call proves one thing: he definitely *is* that desperate.

Maybe, he tries to convince himself, it's just a question of tone. Maybe he can still salvage it. Maybe it'll all be slightly less unbearable if he can bring himself to create a kind of mash-up and season this wretched forced optimism with a pinch of his good old skepticism.

He borrows scissors and Scotch tape from an obliging librarian and pulls the thin sheaf of papers with his notes and fragments from his backpack. Page by page, he searches for sentences he can use, here and there he finds an entire paragraph that still seems workable, and one or another of his formulations even inspires a bit of hope.

With the scissors he cuts what is usable from the manuscript and spreads the snippets out before him, arranged thematically. Then he starts cutting up the pages he's just filled with writing. For a while he moves the fragments here and there on the tabletop, searching for a meaningful order. This, he mutters to himself, needs to be at the beginning . . . and then I can bring in Schopenhauer . . . He painstakingly searches for the edge of the roll of adhesive tape with his fingernail, scratches at it, tears off a piece with his teeth, and sticks Schopenhauer right on the scrap he's chosen for the opening. For a while, things go smoothly. Kraft snips and splices, struggles with the tape, and is filled with optimism at the sight of something completely new and tangible taking shape before him—until he manages to rip a patch of skin from his lip with the Scotch tape. Alarmed, he kneads the painful spot between thumb and forefinger, glances up and becomes aware that all the heads in the reading room have been raised from their screens and books and are following his battle with his material with incredulous fascination. *What's the problem?* he wants to lob at these young faces that, caught out, turn back to their work; of course he knows the key commands for cut and paste—sometimes thinking has to manifest itself in solid matter, but no, these people long ago lost their sense for the haptic, for the tangible. He even harbors the suspicion that they're afraid of its durability, that only the ephemeral, the digital doesn't threaten them. He, on the other hand, shares Derrida's dream of a fountain pen that also functions as a syringe and leaves an indelible subcutaneous trace of the mind in the body. It's probably this last thought—the realization that he shares a dream with Derrida—that throws him so much off-balance that for the blink of an eye he slips out of his own body and can observe himself from a slightly elevated perspective. What he sees isn't a pretty picture. An aging man—although his hair is still full and curly, he'd like to point out—sitting hunched over his desk, blood dripping from his lip and staining the meager fruits of his work, the crudely taped bricolage of his overstretched intellect, as outrageously fantastical ressentiments of modernity rattle around in his empty skull like rancid peanuts . . . One thing is certain, if Erkner were to see him the way he's just seen himself, plying his scissors and Scotch tape, it would have been goodbye to the million.

Kraft flees to the top of the tower; this time he's not seeking refuge from the vacuum cleaner and its Mexican housekeeper, but from himself, so his flight is in vain. It's hot on the observation platform and uncomfortably bright. Kraft stands at the grille on the north side, shades his eyes from the sun, and looks for the skyline on the bay in the distance. The trembling California sun reflects off the distant glass facades and produces a pulsating mist that makes him dizzy. Kraft closes his eyes and traces the yellow reflections that writhe like worms in the obscurity. Ah, Johanna, what did I do to make you so furious?

And suddenly it seems to him as if he's been dragging this question behind him all these years like a prisoner his ball and chain, and as if it alone has prevented him from walking with the fox's fleet-footed gait, the springy step that radiates all necessary optimism.

c
h
a
p
t
e
r
thirteen

Where force does not suffice, ruse steps in.

—PIETRO METASTASIO

kraft is glad that he has a story to tell.

He wouldn't have dared duck Heike's call one more time. Sooner or later he had to answer. After years of employing various strategies of evasion, dishonesty, and repression with Heike, he has learned that telling his lies as soon as possible in the process was an especially effective technique. When Kraft decides on a course of action that he must keep from Heike for tactical reasons, experience has taught him that an early lie is a more credible lie. Best of all is to establish his falsehood even before he acts, because then he can persuade himself, even as he lies, that he can still turn his fiction into the truth by changing his plan at the very last moment.

In this respect, Heike's call was opportune. He was able to tell her he was sitting on the Caltrain to San Francisco: a tedious experience, he explained, since the train had already come to a complete stop twice between stations, the air-conditioning was broken, and anyhow, the lines and rolling stock are in a state that defies description, but since Ivan had needed to leave early in the morning for San Francisco for a daylong meeting at a cybersecurity firm whose scientific advisory board he's on, Kraft couldn't borrow Ivan's car today, and as a result he's now stuck on the tracks in a sheet-metal carriage without AC. Up to this point, it was all true. Having made his decision, Kraft had descended the book-filled tower, carelessly stuffed his bricolage into his backpack, and caught the first Stanford shuttle bus to the Palo Alto train station, where he stood on a platform almost entirely without shade, wondering if he wasn't old enough to wear a hat after all, because then he would have some relief, and on top of that, he'd look damn good next to this station with its aerodynamic 1940s architecture.

But when Heike inevitably asks why he's going to San Francisco, Kraft claims he'll continue on to Berkeley to consult some notebooks in the archives of a long-dead philosopher of science, a lie that came easily to him since in San Francisco he could still decide, instead of looking for Johanna, to change to BART and ride it, under the bay, to Berkeley. For now, it was merely the description of a possibility he could still turn into a reality—even if he didn't have the slightest intention of doing so—and thus it wasn't really a lie.

All the same, he's glad he has a story to tell and to distract him from the real reason for his trip. Caltrain in general, he hastens to add, is a peculiar organization. After waiting for a long time on the hot platform, he saw an enormous diesel locomotive with chimneys spewing billows of exhaust filled with dancing flakes of black soot slowly push enormous, two-level chrome wagons into the station, clanging and hooting, before squealing brakes brought it to a stop. The few noticeboards on the platform unfortunately offered insufficient and rather cryptic information as to whether it was an express train or a local with stops at every station, so everyone just boarded the train and stood in the narrow entryways craning their heads as they tried to understand the blaring, garbled announcement coming over the PA. After that, about half the people who had gotten on the train pushed their way back off, asking questions and talking; then they ran along the platform to ask a uniformed conductor. The whole business went on for quite a long time and was repeated at every station.

In any case, with loud hooting and clanging, the train began to move jerkily and Kraft looked for a seat on one of the upper levels that ran along both sides of the wagon like galleries. There was no chance of reading, the train swayed so much and flung the passengers to this side and that, and on top of it all the old-fashioned vehicle made such an infernal noise—it was almost intolerable even inside the car itself. At some point along the way, the train just stopped between stations. An odd collection of office buildings and shopping centers stretched to the right and left. Sweaty conductors in gray shirts with rattling key rings hanging from their belts pushed their heavy bodies wearily through the narrow corridors, feverishly trying to make sense of their radios' incomprehensible squawking. After some ten minutes the train began to move again, clanging on its way, but then, a few minutes later, that was it, the train stopped again in resigned immobility. The scenery outside the window had hardly changed, the same faceless buildings and here and there a testament to the dream of a single-family home in Victorian or Spanish style. Then the air conditioner failed and it soon became unbearably hot, at which point something strange occurred: one of the conductors made an announcement that they were regrettably unable to determine when the train would get moving again or why they had been given the signal to stop because the range of their handheld radios unfortunately wasn't wide enough for the next station to send information. This announcement just reinforced Kraft's feeling that he was trapped in a time machine.

Handheld radios, Kraft snorts. Walkie-talkies! In the middle of Silicon Valley. Somewhere out there was the Google campus, and a few kilometers farther, Apple, and on the other side he could see the Oracle towers. Facebook, Netflix, Tesla, all just a stone's throw away, but at Caltrain they were still using radio transceivers the size of shoeboxes that couldn't even reach the next station. And the joke is, Kraft says to Heike, that in the middle of it all the two of them are having a private conversation an ocean apart with excellent sound quality. Heike listens without a word. She had liked this about Kraft from the very beginning, how precisely and incisively he could speak about the shortcomings of others, and she still enjoys listening to him even if he's only describing a ramshackle Californian rail line. But when he starts to place his observations in a larger political and cultural theoretical context and to philosophize about the discrepancy between the decrepit state of the infrastructure and the technological sophistication of his fellow travelers' personal gadgets, she quickly loses patience and ends the conversation by mentioning an imminent meeting. She knew what was coming. Lately Kraft has been making particularly critical comments about the effects of privatization, out of character for him, and has even gone so far as to express open approval of greater government support, even if it means raising taxes. She wants none of that. In such moments, Kraft seems to be mellowing with age, and Heike has no time for age or leniency.

a t some point—steaming in his own juices, Kraft has lost all sense of time—the train starts up again and the diesel locomotive pushes the wagons like oversize ovens past the auto body and automotive paint shops that line the tracks in San Bruno, alternating with shabby wooden houses with old sofas rotting next to cars propped up on concrete blocks and worn-out children's trampolines in their parched yards.

In San Francisco he gives the taxi driver the address he found on the website of an association whose members meet regularly in their free time to eradicate the invasive plant species that are killing off the native flora of Northern California. The contact address given was that of a certain Johanna Heuffel, who lived on the corner of Folsom and Stoneman, and Kraft hopes it's the same Johanna, because of whom even today the smell of baking pastries fills him with an emotion he finds hard to place, a conflicted mixture of lovelorn melancholy and plaintive sentimentality, of nebulous guilt and shadowy innocence.

The air-conditioning in the taxi dries his shirt, leaving behind faint clouds of salt on the light blue fabric. He gets out of the car on a steep street, in the shade of elm trees that tower over the tiny wooden houses. Heart beating wildly and ears burning, Kraft looks at the mint-green facade, checks the bay window for signs of life, and eyes the wooden staircase, the brown front door decorated with a bouquet of dried flowers. Just when he's made up his mind and starts to climb the stairs, the door of the adjacent pink house opens and out steps an elderly woman in checked flannel pajamas, her puffy face crowned by an extravagant turban and sporting a nasal oxygen cannula, the tubes of which disappear into an Indian shoulder bag. On a leash, she leads an animal, and Kraft, who's never had much of an interest in zoology, can't tell if it's a young ocelot or a house cat. The woman and the creature examine Kraft with interest and a not-unfriendly air. The animal sidles up to him in a long-legged prance, the woman lets it lead, and Kraft takes a step back. No need to worry, the woman reassures him, Tabby just wants to smell you. So Kraft lets it sniff the backs of his knees, which the animal can reach without stretching, and as it sniffs, Kraft asks about the cat, since he's never seen one like it, either of that size or with such predatory markings. It's an easy conversation to start, because on the one hand he's always happy to learn something new and is already picturing himself telling the twins about the animal and describing its elegant gait, and then, on the other, he's happy to delay the encounter with Johanna a bit longer. Maybe he can find out about her living situation from her neighbor—should he expect to meet a husband, are or were there children?

The woman in the turban, which Kraft assumes conceals a bald head, because her eyebrows consist of two unsteadily drawn arcs and her eyelashes are missing, is happy to provide information. Tabby is a Savannah cat, a cross between a serval, an African wild cat, and a domestic cat. Then the woman launches into a long lecture on breeding difficulties, on F1 to F5 generations, hybrids, characteristics, and prices, which strike Kraft as indecently high for a house pet and immediately make clear to him why the animal is only allowed outside on a leash. He bends down, fondles Tabby's striped ears, repeats several times how interesting it all is, and asks if a Johanna Heuffel lives in the house next door. Yes, the woman confirms, someone by that name does live there, and because Kraft believes he detects a hint of mistrust, he scratches Tabby's chin as well and explains that he's known Johanna since they were students but does not elaborate on the nature of their friendship. Anyhow, he's in San Francisco on business—at Stanford University, actually, he adds, hoping to win her confidence with the university's illustrious name—and he decided to pay a visit to his old friend, whom he hasn't seen since she left Germany.

The neighbor is deeply moved by this story, which Kraft embellishes with a few well-targeted exotic details from the Swiss border city and long trips through East and West Germany, and she tells him regretfully that sadly he won't find Joan here. They own a house in Sonoma County, on the coast, and spend most of their time there. The third-person plural roars in Kraft's ears but he doesn't dare ask why she uses it. And why should he, was he such a fool to think that Johanna had waited for him all these years?

h e rents a car downtown. ESCAPE is written on the back. Is our man Kraft on the run? Isn't it rather the opposite? Does he not finally want to face something he's been fleeing for thirty years? Kraft himself isn't sure, and when he sits down behind the steering wheel of the oversize vehicle, he no longer knows why it was so important to see Johanna. What on earth is he doing here?

Kraft enters the address he got from the neighbor into the car's GPS and leaves navigation to the friendly female voice. *Follow Fourth Street, then turn right on Harrison. Now turn right.* Actually, he had thought he would leave the city on the Golden Gate, but the GPS has chosen the Bay Bridge instead. It seems to be the shorter route. So be it, he didn't come here to play the tourist and it's nice to let someone else make the decisions. For the first time, he understands the appeal of driverless cars. He'd never understood all the hype. Who wants to be driven around by a computer, to hand over the reins? he'd always wondered. He certainly wouldn't, he could barely stand sitting in the passenger seat. But now he would gladly let go of the steering wheel and put himself in the hands of this friendly voice. Maybe she knows what he does not: this whole trip isn't leading anywhere good. Maybe she knows where he should really be headed. Maybe she might, quite intentionally, ignore the bridge's gentle curve and, together with Kraft, crash straight through the white railing and vault in a high arc over the bay's blue water.

Kraft crosses another bridge, drives past a large prison, through industrial zones, and down streets filled with shopping centers. He passes small towns, villages, and residential areas, drives through marshes and grasslands, guided by the friendly voice, now right, now left, often straight ahead. She leads him northward, always northward, then she tells him to take another left and an immediate right, and Kraft passes vineyards, burned grasslands, isolated farms, and red barns. Fences and telephone wires line the roads, the hills roll gently, and the cattle chew stoically. The bushes grow more densely, now and again a small coniferous forest offers a little shade, the colors change, more green, one with a silvery sheen and one the same shade as the Neckar River, sometimes a red the color of the tile roofs in Tübingen appears, and a yellow like lichen. Kraft smells the ocean long before he sees it. After Bodega Bay, the road follows the coast. At Duncans Landing he turns off into a rest stop and stares out the open window at the rough water, trying in vain to feel an appropriate emotion, and his companion loses patience: *Turn around and follow the Shoreline Highway.* Kraft obeys. At some point, just before Russian River, he is told to turn left, toward the Pacific, and then right, up a small hill with individual homes, their verandas bleached by the sun, dotting its flank. Kraft parks behind one of the houses next to a

Toyota Prius. *You have reached your destination*, the voice tells him, and sets Kraft to brooding about the English language and the shared etymology of *destiny* and *destination*, which doesn't exist in German, but the thought doesn't lead anywhere and he has no choice but to turn off the motor and get out of the car.

Johanna's house makes an effort to blend into the landscape. It huddles in a pine forest brushed by the wind. From the road, only a rough weather-beaten plank wall is visible, windowless and gray. Through a gap in the wall, Kraft slips into an inner courtyard of monastic severity. Moss and bamboo, a rustic birdbath of Japanese stoneware, a path paved with slate slabs leads him to the door. Kraft rings the bell, listens, peeks through the narrow window next to the door, and wipes the palms of his hands dry on his trousers one more time. Johanna, Johanna . . . She opens the door.

The same haircut, as if it had been trimmed with kitchen scissors, but completely white now, the same narrow shoulders, and she still wears boat shoes. Yes, she says, how can I help you? Kraft has to clear his throat. It's me, Richard.

Good Lord, she cries in a hoarse voice, Richard! Richard Kraft! Closely watching her reaction, he mainly sees surprise. To his relief and to his astonishment he sees no trace of anger. Her surprise quickly gives way to a heartiness Kraft distrusts because it seems very American. An impression that is reinforced by the strong English coloring her Swabian has taken on over the decades. Words tumble awkwardly from her mouth, as if her slender face were too small for them.

Kraft is invited into her house, its interior bearing no trace of the courtyard's simplicity. He follows her through spacious rooms with views of the Pacific out large picture windows. She leads him to a big kitchen with laminated-wood cabinetry and a central island, offers him an iced tea, and while she fills two glasses and decorates them with sprigs of mint, Kraft stiffens, because he has the feeling that this is the moment she will ask after the reason for his visit. Instead she turns to face him and switches back into English. What a surprise, she says, and Kraft notices that her skin, which he remembers as pale and fine and prone to rashes, has been saturated by the California sun and taken on a leathery tan. He's still searching for a sign of disappointment or bitterness, of burgeoning rage provoked by his appearance, but Johanna seems as relaxed as the large, shaggy sheepdog stretched out on the terrace doorstep, over which she steps agilely.

Come, she says, and Kraft follows her clumsily because the knee that got battered during his rowing adventure has started to ache again. He feels unsteady on his feet in general, as if he were standing for the first time after a long illness. As he takes a large step over the sleeping dog, he's struck by a wave of dizziness and has to grab on to the doorframe. The dog opens one eye briefly and thumps its tail on the floor. Mimi, Johanna says, we have an unexpected guest.

Mimi, a heavyset woman in cargo shorts, a tank top, and sandals closes her issue of *The New York Review of Books* and rises from her wooden reclining chair. Is this why the neighbor used the plural? Kraft wonders. Mimi, this is Richard, an old friend from Germany. From my time in Basel, she specifies. Mimi pushes her sunglasses into her thick white curls and offers her hand. Oh, she says, looking at Johanna, this is who tried to seduce you with *On the Marble Cliffs*? A moment of silence follows and Kraft is sure the question will come now. He feels nauseated and is worried his legs will buckle.

Sit, sit, Mimi says, and points to one of the white wooden chairs. Kraft gratefully sinks into the chair and sets his iced tea on the broad armrest, glad that he can stop the nervous clinking of the ice cubes. He looks around admiringly. Beautiful, he says, amazing, the house, the garden, the view, the ocean, very beautiful, and he points at each thing as he names it as if he has to inform the women what there is to see.

But now, Johanna begins, tell us—now, right now, she's going to ask the question he will have to parry with another question, one for which he may prefer not to have an answer . . . and anyway, what could he possibly say? Johanna, Johanna, how did I make you so angry?—how did you find us? Oh, that one he can answer! Happy for the reprieve, he goes into great detail about the website on which he found their address in San Francisco—alien plant species, very interesting, he'd like to hear more about that later—and how he didn't find Johanna there—obviously, he adds with a nervous laugh—but he did meet a neighbor with a gigantic cat, about the size of a lynx, it was on a leash and the woman was friendly enough to give him their address. Oh, Mimi says, that's Joyce and her cat Tabby. Then . . . another moment of silence.

The dog yawns. Mimi sighs. She doesn't have much longer to live. Kraft expresses his regret and says that she didn't give that impression, quite the contrary, in fact, since she had sniffed the backs of his knees enthusiastically and was very lively. Oh, no, not the cat, Joyce, Mimi corrects him. Ah, Kraft says, of course, she had an oxygen tank with her. Cancer, Mimi says. And we're going to inherit the cat, Johanna sighs, a ten-thousand-dollar cat you have to keep on a leash and feed special food flown in from Denmark, and the vet she needs to see once a month is in Fresno. But they promised Joyce that they would take care of Tabby after her death. Johanna gives a shrug of resignation and her laughter is at once so bright and so hoarse that for a moment Kraft feels transported back thirty years to an attic apartment in Basel.

Kraft sips his iced tea. Now that he's seated, he feels a bit stronger and decides to gain time by going on the offensive and asks Johanna bluntly how things have gone for her all these years. After lighting a cigarette, she tells him with good grace that she worked several years for the biotech company for which she had left Basel back then and then founded a gene-sequencing software company with two partners in the late '90s. The dot-com bubble almost did them in, but business recovered and three years ago they sold the company to a large corporation and she retired, so to speak. And now, she says, we're sitting here with more money than two old girls like us can possibly spend in the years we have left.

Kids? Kraft is bold enough to ask, feeling very progressive because he thinks the question will show him to be particularly open-minded about their lifestyle, which does surprise him somewhat, perhaps even unnerves him. No, Johanna waves the question away, no kids, but we have the dog. Kraft isn't sure if she means this seriously; her smile is so mischievous, perhaps even mocking. And instead of asking Kraft about his life, she offers to show him the beach as if she suspects he has something he would rather discuss with her alone.

Johanna goes into the house to get a leash, at the sight of which the dog jumps up eagerly. A steep footpath leads down to the ocean. The dog runs ahead, Johanna follows easily, and Kraft makes an effort to keep up.

Kraft feels stunned, defeated. Unused to driving such a big car, he can hardly stay in his lane. He's turned off the friendly female voice and is driving south somewhat haphazardly; as long as he keeps the Pacific to his right, he'll reach San Francisco somehow. But what for? Right . . . he has to return the rental car. The road winds its way down in sweeping curves, past tsunami warning signs and parking areas with young people sitting on the tailgates of their pickups, their neoprene suits rolled down to their hips, then it climbs again in switchbacks along steep cliffs. How long has he been driving? He doesn't know. Kraft can't feel anything below his hips, but his feet do their duty, accelerating and braking on their own. His ears, on the other hand, burn with shame. They hang from his skull like pulsating slabs of meat while a storm rages in their sinuous canals.

J ohanna had energetically waved the insects away from a pile of rotten kelp and pulled from the organic mess a tubular stalk with a fist-size air bladder on one end. She twirled it over her head and launched it into the rough surf. The dog leaped after it. So, she asked, what brings you here?

Kraft began telling her about his invitation to Stanford, explained the essay competition, elucidated the problematics of the topic, described Erkner, but Johanna didn't let him off, interrupted his account, and asked to know what had brought him here, to her? Were you hoping to find an answer to the theodicy questions? Kraft laughed nervously. Well, yes, in a way . . . that is . . . at least, she was right in thinking he had come to her with a question. Johanna bent down to the stalk of seaweed the dog had laid at her feet and flung it back into the waves. Shoot! she prompted him, and gave an encouraging look. Well, Kraft answered, he was afraid he no longer knew why the question had seemed so important, but since he was here . . . then, fine . . . he had urgently needed to know, for reasons that were hard to describe, what it was he'd done, back then in June of '87, to make her so angry that she left for America and disappeared forever.

Johanna was visibly perplexed. She didn't understand the question, she said. Well, that is, Kraft offered . . . he knew it was his job to remember why and he was perfectly aware that this gap in his memory didn't put him in the best light, but maybe that was exactly why it was so important?

But Richard, she said, I honestly have no idea what you're talking about. Your rage . . . Kraft insisted, what did I do that made you so angry? She was never angry, she assured him, she didn't have the slightest idea what he was talking about. But she did throw her clothes in a suitcase and slam the door behind her, after all . . .

Johanna was silent for a moment. Is that really how he remembers it? she wanted to know. Kraft nodded mutely. Interesting, because she was confident that he was the one who, in a fit of rage, threw his books and his clothes into two suitcases and slammed the door behind him. Kraft stared into the milky bank of clouds that lay over the water on the horizon as if hoping the past would reveal itself there and give the lie to Johanna's version.

But . . . he began again before lapsing into silence. After she got her doctorate, she was offered a position in San Francisco, Johanna reminded him, speaking to him like an intractable patient, and it was out of the question that she refuse it and it had been perfectly clear to her that he wouldn't follow her since his professional future lay in Germany. To her surprise he had then told her his dream of starting a family with her, and today, with distance, she had to admit that it must have been very vexing to him that she didn't take his dream seriously, and the obvious misunderstanding, or more precisely, the asymmetry that had underlain their relationship from the beginning must have then become crystal clear. He was hurt and, yes, furious, downright furious. But she, and she's sorry she has to admit it at this point, went off to America with a light heart and without the slightest rancor, delighted to be starting a new phase in her life. Johanna bent down again for the seaweed and flung it into the Pacific.

Kraft watched the spinning object as it soared and splashed into the ocean. She just throws everything away, without a second thought, he reflected.

After this, there wasn't much left to say and they climbed the steep path in single file. Johanna walked him to his car and after he was seated behind the wheel and she lobbed a "drive safely" through the window he reared up one last time and had the presumption to ask if he was the one who had turned her off men. Johanna burst into laughter. Oh, my dear Kraft, she said, you weren't really that bad . . .

. . . and above all not that important. Did she really say that? Or was that just how he heard it? When the red pylons and the white city in the hills behind them appear, he's no longer sure exactly how things went. He parks the car in the lot at the entrance to the bridge, walks under the bridge, and climbs to the lookout. Under normal circumstances he would avoid this kind of place, filled with mobile homes, noisy families, and so many cameras, but the visit to Johanna's had completely spun him around, and now the sum of his misanthropic resources was concentrated on himself, as if he were the last man alive and therefore the only one left to hate.

Kraft stands in the crowd of tourists and, one sheep in a herd, looks up at the Golden Gate, that elegant bridge over which endless streams of traffic flow in both directions, and at the islands in the bay, Angel Island, almost at his feet, and behind it Alcatraz, where evil had once been locked away.

So, then, can he no longer trust his own memory? Had he been mistaken? Like with the robin redbreasts? Maybe, in the tower filled with books on war, revolution, and peace, there's a reference work called *All About Kraft*, in which he can read about how things really went.

And how about with Ruth? Is his memory faulty there, too? No, there we can assume things really did happen as he remembers them.

K raft was at a conference in the Canadian Rocky Mountains and so Ruth had a few days of peace and quiet in the Tübingen apartment with a view of the Stift and the Hölderlin Tower for the first time since she had left Berlin four years earlier. Daniel, who'd just started his first year of high school, was away for a few days on a class trip to the Black Forest, and Adam (yes, Kraft had prevailed in the choice of names—he'd claimed it was his right since he'd been so shamefully disregarded with his first son and Ruth had little to say in her defense, especially since she was thankful that he had accepted her veto of Otto), Adam, then, was finally in kindergarten. So now, because Kraft was traveling and had taken the hectic hustle and bustle he cultivated whenever he was home for a few hours in order to emphasize his entitlement, despite his frequent absences, to his role as head of the family, with him to the Canadian mountains, where he could plague his colleagues with it, a heavenly calm reigned in the rooms with French doors, gleaming parquet flooring, and the stucco of Protestant dignity. Ruth spent the first three days stretched out on the couch, with her eyes closed and a book on her stomach, searching the silence for her lost strength, and listening to her own breath, which she hadn't heard for a long time. On the fourth day, she rose, threw the unread book on the floor, and climbed the narrow flight of stairs to the attic. She was greeted by a suffocating, unbearably dry heat. The late-summer sun streamed through the large skylights and baked the tiles, and the hot roof beams gave off a musty smell of old fir wood. Big rolls of wool insulation were piled behind the door. Kraft had ordered them four years earlier, but had always found one more talk he had to write, one more lecture he had to prepare, one more set of proofs he had to read over immediately, a pile of term papers to correct, all sorts of reasons why he wasn't able to take up the promised construction—much to his regret, as he occasionally added when the topic came up, because he could certainly see how exciting it would be if Ruth were able to enrich their family life with her art. In fact, he especially enjoyed having a woman at his side at social events whom he could introduce as a sculptor from Berlin and thus bring a hint of Bohemia to dowdy Tübingen academic circles, although he was naturally aware that it was primarily due to his own ambition and egoism that Ruth hadn't touched a file, a chisel, or a lump of clay since the day she'd moved in.

Ruth pushed to the side a few discarded toys and some winter sports equipment that had been carelessly piled in the storage space and walked past the long row of BILLY shelving on which Kraft had—only temporarily, mind you—placed the books for which there was no room in his office. She searched all the way in the back for the boxes containing her art supplies. A large bag of clay slabs lay on top of them, baked by the heat of the uninsulated attic into useless tiles. Ruth stood looking at them for a long time then spun energetically on her heel without opening a single box; she climbed back down to the silent apartment, looked for a thick marker, packing tape, and paper, returned to the attic, and wrote the address of a friend's studio in Berlin on the boxes. On her way down, she grabbed a few empty moving boxes and two large suitcases. She began packing hurriedly. She was afraid she would lose her courage and determination when Adam got home from kindergarten because Adam was just like his father, a big chatterbox, had been since day one, a babbler and blatherer, who started talking unconscionably early, forming sentences, asking questions he would answer himself, exuding knowledge as soon as he acquired it, and accompanying the day-to-day of his childish life with an unquenchable torrent of noises, words, and sentences, as if he were providing commentary for a football game. But it would be a mistake to assume that Kraft appreciated this quality in his son. In fact, it seemed to Ruth that Kraft was more inclined to compete with his son for the last word and felt challenged in a field that was once his alone because his firstborn son, driven into inner emigration by Ackerknecht and the representations of his dead daughter, had not found his voice again in Tübingen and remained a pale, silent child, with whom Kraft never was able to connect, despite his sincere efforts whenever he found the time.

Ruth let her friend in Berlin know she was coming, handed the smaller of the two suitcases to her older son when he returned from his class trip, before he'd even taken off his backpack, took Adam's hand with her left hand and the other suitcase with her right and disappeared to Berlin forever.

When Kraft arrived home, he found a note on the kitchen table asking him to let the moving company she had hired into the apartment and to make sure they took the boxes with her sculpting tools, and he felt such a strong sense of relief that the bursting of his bourgeois dreams didn't upset him for the time being.

We may well assume that his momentary relief sprang from the euphoria the days in the Rocky Mountains had inspired in him and that the collapse of his marriage and his family's departure appeared to him as a liberation and the new start he'd been yearning for.

after Ivan had leaped down from the Wall on the Brandenburg Gate side and Kraft on the Tiergarten side, they didn't have any news of each other for a long time. Kraft had written Ivan a letter in which he tried to explain in great detail his relationship to the gerbera-wielding Lambsdorff, but whereas he could usually find an explanation for almost anything—at least in those days when he felt the winds of history beneath his wings—this proved particularly difficult for him. He didn't receive an answer. Only a few months later, when Kraft needed a best man and couldn't think of anyone other than István Pánczél, whom he couldn't possibly ask, for obvious reasons, did it become painfully clear to him how much he missed his friend.

Eventually chance forced the two of them to end their silence. Ivan, who risked being pushed to the margins of academia by the course of world events, remembered the philosophical studies he had neglected in the previous years and resumed teaching and publishing in the field. Independently of each other, they both agreed to join the editorial staff of a newly founded scholarly journal and in the course of this work, they were forced to engage in sporadic e-mail correspondence, which was at first limited to purely professional matters but soon expanded to include brief postscripts of a personal nature: the announcement of McKenzie's birth, a terse notice of the death of Kraft's mother, the publication of a book . . .

The conference in the Rocky Mountains was the first occasion on which they met in person after the rupture. Kraft felt ambivalent about the reunion. He was looking forward to seeing Ivan, but at the same time, Kraft was worried that his friend would demand accountability for his shabby behavior in the days when he, István, lay in the Berlin clinic, fighting for his sight. But then the conference was a triumph, from every point of view.

An extremely ambitious staff member at NATO's science program had organized this small and very exclusive panel on the rhetoric of disarmament for which an eclectic group of high NATO officials, diplomats, politicians, and military officers decorated with stars and golden fourragères were confined under high security to a winter sports hotel deserted in the off-season. As for Kraft, he owed his invitation to a slightly less ambitious staff member of the Federal Foreign Office's Science and Technology Committee who had been charged with finding an appropriate German scholar for the conference but who couldn't decide what would be appropriate based on the conference title and thus, for the sake of simplicity, assumed that a chaired professor of rhetoric must surely be a suitable candidate, an assumption Kraft did not contest, happy for any opportunity to escape his family.

From the very first day, Ivan went all out and made a vocal and voluble case for a rhetoric of victors, because the velvet gloves that were now in vogue irritated him no end. He even went so far as to accuse his colleagues of having a taste for blandishment as far as their defeated foes, something he, who had suffered the effects of communism firsthand, considered completely unacceptable. He did not share their understanding of the Russians' concern about the threat of an eastward NATO expansion and he admonished the participants again and again to keep their eyes on China and to not believe that Cuba was finished.

Kraft immediately rallied to Ivan's side, out of equal parts conviction and the hope that he could make amends and restore their old bonds of friendship. Together they got on their colleagues' nerves by contradicting them nonstop with historical arguments they seemed to have at hand by the sackful, studies they could cite by the paragraph, complete with all the proper figures, and with recourse, when necessary, to obscure theorists no one but the two of them had ever heard of. In the evenings they sat on a terrace of pinewood, a bit apart from the group, looking at the Canadian forests, threaded with brown lanes and inoperative ski lifts, and drinking Crown Royal and ginger ale, reveling in memories of the old days in Berlin, thereby gracefully avoiding sensitive topics. Once in a while, an aging Italian rear admiral in a chic white uniform sat with them and listened to their conversation with a pensive smile, not understanding a word they said, but this soldier of the Cold War saw in these two valiant young men a future he had believed lost.

fourteen

If a man has not made a million dollars by the time he is forty, he is not worth much.

—HERBERT HOOVER

if we know, then, that Kraft's recollection of the end of his relationship with Ruth is correct, we have an advantage over him, because he stands there, looking into the distance, completely unsure whether he can still trust his memory. The ground sways beneath his feet and screams reach him from some distant world.

All around him, people are running and shouting. The

tourists are toppling like bowling pins, holding tight to their cameras. Kraft drops to the ground as well, he falls to his knees like a sinner, then farther forward, but the ground, on which he tries to brace himself with outstretched arms, is trembling and offers him no support. His arms give way, his forehead knocks against the asphalt, and he ends up flat on his stomach. Then our Kraft raises his chin and watches incredulously as the bridge before him is seized with a fit of trembling. A jolt sends a wave through the road that makes the cars hop like toys, followed by another that twists the bridge grotesquely, makes it whip even higher, and tosses the cars over the railing as if shaking off pesky insects as its steel beams groan and cables buzz and snap with the sound of overstretched guitar strings. Beams break, and with a bang the red bridge splinters and falls into the bay, which rises up roaring as the houses on the opposite shore begin to dance. The tip of the Transamerica Pyramid sways, the entire building spins halfway around its own axis and collapses with the grace of a lady in the Portuguese court. The city seems to be sliding, the grid of streets is thrown off-kilter, the high-rises on Market Street crumble, dragging each other into ruin and sending up a cloud of dust over the hills. The shaking and trembling doesn't let up, and Kraft, still lying face-down, feels the earth's rage spread up through his guts.

After an eternity of minutes, the ground stops shaking, dust rains onto Kraft's back, and through the screams of the wounded and the parents' calls for their lost children, hundreds of car alarms blare from the parking lot. Kraft stands up, staggers, runs panic-stricken past the weeping and wailing and those trapped between the bodies of cars. A man stops him, clamps his hands on Kraft's shoulders, and begs for help, pointing at his wife, who is lying on her back, legs outspread, crushed beneath the bronze statue of a sailor that's fallen from its plinth and fatally violated her through the force of physics alone.

Help me, help me! the man croaks, shaking Kraft as if to wake him from a nightmare. With one look at the woman's crushed chest and protruding intestines, Kraft sees that she is beyond help and as if this appalling sight restores his sense of reason, he stops for a moment and calls his friend through the chaos: István, István.

Kraft turns on his heel, runs back to the lookout point, climbs over the crumbled stone wall, and searches for a path down to the bay. Avoiding the landslides and leaping over deep fissures in the asphalt, he stumbles more than runs to where boats float capsized or are piled together in a chaotic mess on dry land. Kraft finds an intact rubber dinghy amid the wreck of a pier, its motor chugging, its owner no doubt floating out in the rough water with his head split open. Kraft jumps on board and steers toward the city in rubble.

At the Ferry Building, or what's left of it—in falling, the tower smashed the deck of a ferry docked at the pier—Kraft goes on land. Half of the Hyatt Hotel's facade has crashed onto Market Street and Kraft looks into the gaping lobby as if into the depths of a Gursky photograph. The lightly injured carry the severely injured, survivors throw themselves on the corpses of their loved ones, and the bewildered huddle in groups and pray. Dust hangs in the air along with the smell of bricks and cement. Sirens wail by the thousands. Kraft knows he doesn't have much time before the giant, all-devouring wave washes over the Golden Gate and engulfs the bay. Scaling rubble and dodging sprays of sparks from loose wires, ignoring the tohubohu around him, he hurries to the spot where he assumes the building would be, in which his friend works upstairs. Beams twisted grotesquely, chunks of concrete with protruding rebar, and millions of shards of green reflecting glass are strewn where the proud Clause-VRiX Inc. tower stood. At Kraft's feet lie the shattered remains of the neon logo with the cross pattée and not far off is a heavy oak conference table on which debris is piled. Kraft finds his friend half-buried underneath it. He stretches out beside the groaning man and brushes the hair from his forehead. Everything will be fine, István, it will all be fine. Using every ounce of his strength, he pulls his friend out from under the table, uninjured.

Kraft sets a fallen motorcycle upright, swings himself onto the seat, Ivan sits behind him and wraps his abraded arms around his friend. They roar up Market Street in a wild zigzag, fires burn to the right and left, and looters climb into the Apple store through the jagged windows. Nearby, the first shots ring out.

They have to get to high ground before the water comes. But Kraft still has to take care of one more thing. He makes a sharp turn onto Folsom Street, entire blocks are in flames, the old wooden houses blaze like kindling. He drives higher and higher at breakneck speed until he can go no farther. Uprooted elms block the road. Kraft and Ivan jump off the bike, scramble over the trunks, clear a way through the leaves and roots.

They come to a stop, panting, in front of the ruins of a small pink house. Tabby, Kraft calls, Tabby! The branches of an elm protrude from the broken windows and the roof, caved in by the trunk, sags deeply between the cracked walls. Kraft yanks open the front door. Joyce lies facedown on the living room floor, her turban has slipped off to reveal a gaping wound in her bald head; a roof beam has brought her salvation. Tabby sits between Joyce's thin shoulder blades, playing with the plastic tube of the cannula. Kraft grabs the cat, holds it tight against his chest, and leaves the scene of horror. Higher, ever higher, they run up the grassy Bernal Heights hill.

Thousands upon thousands of San Franciscans, injured and

unscathed—some have even carried the corpses of their loved ones over the protests of the living– stand on the hill, gazes fixed toward the north, from which they expect the deadly wall of water to come.

The cat stiffens in Kraft's arms, its ears twitch and swivel like parabolic antennae toward the Golden Gate. Groaning and wailing spreads through the crowd as the white crest of the wave appears on the horizon, spreads out to the sides, and rolls through the bay, dragging everything with it, shoving the debris of the city far inland. With a roaring and crashing that can be heard on the top of the hill, the wave destroys everything in its path that had withstood the earthquake.

Still holding the cat, Kraft pushes his way with Ivan through the survivors to the south side of the hill and from there they watch the wave as it buries Silicon Valley beneath it, expands the bay, and washes water up to the foot of the mountains. They see the start-ups and tech companies, the staid industrial buildings, and the rubble of the glass office buildings being swept away to the south toward the campus of Stanford University. The tower filled with books on war, revolution, and peace withstands the approaching mass of water for a disappointing moment, but then gives way, breaks apart, and releases its accumulated knowledge. There goes the conference, Kraft says to himself . . .

He opens his eyes: the red bridge before him, the Transamerica Pyramid upright on the opposite side of the bay, and the tourist taking photographs. No, the city would never do him that favor. Kraft returns to his car, noses into the rush-hour traffic, and crosses the bridge. He has to return the rental car.

things don't look good for Kraft. He has exactly twenty-four hours before the start of the conference and he is farther from finding an answer to the prize question than he was three weeks ago, when he was wrestling with a package of wasabi peas thirty thousand feet over Arkansas and his triumph over the recalcitrant foil package brought with it a certainty of victory he believed he was entitled to, given his intellectual superiority.

An hour ago, he had opened PowerPoint and searched for Tübingen University's presentation template, which his secretary had installed for him. Maybe that's the right path, since there's no time left to write a polished lecture; just fill in a few slides with sonorous bullet points and improvise from there. But since his visit to Johanna, he's been carrying around a sense of shame that inhibits all larger thoughts and restricts the soaring flight of his intellect, on which he otherwise could always rely, to a timid circling around her parting words—like a housefly on a stovetop, Kraft thinks.

b ut isn't it past time to ask ourselves why Kraft's financial situation has been mentioned on at least a couple of occasions as being among the reasons he finds himself unable to write, and from which we then deduced, in combination with his family situation, the existential necessity for him to impress the jury—that is, Tobias Erkner in particular? Are Kraft's finances in such a terrible state that Heike will only agree to a divorce if he brings home the million dollars because she's worried that she won't be able to provide adequately for herself and the twins? Such is, in fact, the case, although Kraft brings home a respectable monthly salary as a full professor and in some months Heike herself—depending on the assignment flow at her higher-ed consulting firm, which she founded shortly after the birth of the twins—contributes as much or even more to the family income.

We must look much further in the past for the source of the problem, back to the moment when Ruth took her youngest son by the hand and disappeared with both boys to Berlin for good, since although Kraft sat down after reading her letter, opened a bottle of wine, and toasted both his restored friendship with Ivan as well as his new freedom, and didn't have a single thought to spare for Ruth or his two sons, at least not on that evening, it would be too easy to see him as a monster without a conscience, especially since he saw himself as an honorable man and commissioned a lawyer the very next morning to draw up an alimony agreement with Ruth so that she and their sons would be generously supported.

He kept the apartment in Tübingen—he hadn't yet completely wiped away his dreams of a bourgeois family—took out a second mortgage, and paid out Ruth, who bought herself an apartment and a studio in Berlin, had them insulated by a professional, and, with the money left over, purchased the complete works of Freud, read about half, and finally took up her artistic work again.

When Kraft carried Heike, already pregnant with the twins, across the threshold six years later, it was clear that he had overstretched his resources. The interest on the mortgages and the generous support he still provided for Ruth and his sons ate up his professor's salary month after month. By his mid-forties, he had neither put anything aside nor paid anything off.

Indeed: his sons . . . Adam let his mother take his hand and, completely unaffected by the unusual events, he kept talking. He never looked back, not once, nor was he silent for a single moment during the long train ride to Berlin, instead he began to picture his future in the new city in dazzling colors as if he were hoping to find a larger audience for his monologues there. It never was clear to any of those involved whether Adam missed his father or not. Prattling merrily, he visited Kraft in Tübingen on school holidays, drove to Tuscany or Greece with him, chattering and nattering all the while; and, blathering cheerfully, he left his father behind at the end of the vacation. His relationship with his mother, on the other hand, became increasingly strained because Ruth, after self-medicating with half of Freud, had placed herself in the hands of a gifted therapist who advised her, if she were to feel the old weakness coming on in the presence of a blatherer, to start singing "Hava Nagila," tapping the rhythm out with her index finger on her tragus, the small prominence of cartilage in the middle of the outer ear. When Adam had rambled on as an adolescent, this habit of his mother's led to ever more frequent rows, so Ruth was by no means unhappy when he decided at fourteen to finish his education at a boarding school in England. Ruth willingly sacrificed the small inheritance she had received from an aunt for this undertaking, informed Kraft by telephone, and let him take over the not inconsiderable balance of the tuition fees, under the threat of sending Adam back to Tübingen if he refused. Kraft volubly and eloquently countered this plan, which he denounced as an inappropriate vote of no-confidence in the German educational system, but he quickly acquiesced when he got the impression Ruth was again humming a Jewish folk song at the other end of the line, a strange new habit he found particularly disagreeable and that led Kraft into mistaken doubts regarding his ex-wife's mental health. The English boarding school was thus an additional strain on Kraft's finances, and as he had feared, after Adam had finished his A-levels, the boy naturally felt that German universities too wouldn't be good enough for him, and consequently Kraft had to wire tuition fees in pounds sterling every six months, a burden that continues to the present day with regard to Adam's business school studies. Adam's decision to pursue a business degree of all things was not one to ease the pain of this financial sacrifice, since Kraft considers "businessmen" to be in general nothing more than talented salesmen who've adorned themselves with an academic aura. But Kraft would also have to admit that after Adam's voice changed, his jabbering—to which one could, earlier, with a measure of goodwill, have attributed an innocent, childlike charm—drifted more and more in the direction of carnival barking, and so he happened to fit into his current surroundings very well.

As for Kraft's relationship with his first son, we must unfortunately admit that the ties that bound them in the years when they lived together as a family proved too weak to withstand the seven hundred kilometers between Berlin and Tübingen. Kraft was never able to establish for himself a significant place in his son's life, which we must, in all fairness, point out was not solely attributable to his insufficient level of engagement, but also to the—as he saw it—unhealthy symbiotic relationship that had been established between mother and son due to the lack of a male attachment figure . . . a role Ackerknecht was neither willing nor able to fill.

We can summarize things as follows: Daniel did not need a father, which Kraft willingly conceded—and he paid.

For a while he had tried to share at least in the most important events in his eldest son's life. He traveled to Berlin and sat next to Ruth in the front row at Danny's composition diploma recital at the Berlin Conservatory, for the premiere of a string quartet he had composed. Because Kraft arrived late, he sat on the last bench of the Lutheran church when his son married an evangelic pastor from Cottbus, and he even attended the baptism of his first grandchild in a run-down farmhouse in Brandenburg, where Danny had turned a shed into a small recording studio in which he composed advertisement jingles for a small fee and composed on the side his great concert cycle on the relationship between humans and animals, while his wife organized the Christian resistance out of the parish hall against the neo-Nazi settlers who were moving into the village in large family groups, taking up organic farming on their cheaply bought land, celebrating heathen fire rituals, and declaring the village a "nationally liberated zone." This environment depressed Kraft so deeply that he didn't show up for his second grandchild's baptism, but instead deposited an obolus in an account in the baby's name with the Oder-Spree Savings Bank, something he has done every two years each time yet another birth announcement decorated with a Taizé cross arrived in his mailbox.

Still, no one has to go hungry at the Krafts', not at all. But Kraft himself has to concur with Heike's assessment: a divorce with all the costs entailed in establishing a second household isn't feasible in their current situation, certainly not without a reduction in their cost of living, and she is not remotely prepared to agree to a change in lifestyle. So Heike is right: Erkner's million is the only solution. Kraft knows this, but he is revolted to find that freedom comes with a price.

K raft gets a ham sandwich and a can of Diet Coke in the Green Library café and runs into Bertrand Ducavalier and his perpetual good humor. Ducavalier beams at the sight of Kraft and insists on joining him on his bench. They haven't seen each other since Bertrand turned his back prematurely on Paris and most particularly on the Rue d'Ulm a few years earlier and withdrew to his family's vineyard in Burgundy, where he watches his sister practice viticulture and leads the life of an independent scholar.

Ivan told Kraft that it had taken all his powers of persuasion to lure Ducavalier to Erkner's conference in California, but of course

Kraft knows how much Bertrand enriches every conference he attends. Kraft can only agree, after all, he not only values Bertrand's lectures and conversational contributions, always a breath of fresh air in the bleakest conferences, but also his qualities as a dining companion. Bertrand has always been able to find the one good restaurant in even the strangest cities, and when there isn't a single good restaurant, then the least bad, and you can be sure that even there he will put together a wonderful evening, because his savoir vivre doesn't have the slightest trace of pomposity. He doesn't need a rare wine—although he's naturally able to find the best (not necessarily the most expensive) bottle in the longest of wine lists—and if there's only a house wine, then a few carafes of it will do. There's no need for extravagant dishes either, yet he is nonetheless able to turn any evening into a banquet and a feast. Kraft knows why that is: Ducavalier's savoir vivre is not inborn—Kraft doesn't believe in that kind of thing—but is something that was inculcated in him from day one, he was immersed in it his entire childhood and adolescence; it became second nature, but because he's an intelligent and thoughtful man, he also knows that it is a privilege he has done nothing to earn, it was endowed on him at birth, and that is precisely why he has such a relaxed approach to it. It's also why Kraft can deeply envy his ease and his savoir vivre and admire it at the same time, something he's otherwise only able to do with dead men or Margaret Thatcher. He admires Bertrand's charm, his somewhat threadbare elegance, which always seems fortuitous. His white shirts made from fabric both sturdy and soft that look like he must have inherited them from his father. His always rather worn shoes, rarely freshly polished, still look more elegant than Kraft's carefully waxed Budapesters. What he admires most about Bertrand, however, is that for all his ease and suavity in matters of lifestyle, he still remains an inveterate leftist and outspoken polemicist.

Kraft recalls that evening in Sarajevo, when several participants of a conference had happily followed Bertrand into a cellar restaurant; after a lengthy meal, he had pulled a cigarette from his shirt pocket and explained why he had decided to leave the École Normale Supérieure on the Rue d'Ulm. He had finally understood that he, a scion of a family as old as it was rich, who had of course been educated in the very best schools and who had resolutely carried the banner of the working class on his predetermined march through the institutions, was part of France's problem and could not, as he had long been convinced, also be part of the solution, and he was therefore going to retire to his family's vineyard at the end of the semester. The French left was guilty of two misdeeds—no, it would be more accurate to call them sins. Firstly, they've never seriously attempted to reform France's elitist and neo-feudal educational system—a system of which he himself was, as a graduate of two of the Grandes Écoles, a beneficiary; and as a professor at the Rue d'Ulm he bore some responsibility by training students, year after year, to be a part of this same elitist circus. But now that Hollande, the saddest of those clowns, had stepped into the ring as president, Ducavalier could not and would not take part any longer. It was certainly easy to dismiss Bertrand as an aging cynic resting on his inherited wealth and watching, wineglass in hand, as things went to hell. But Ducavalier saw it as an exercise in humility: admit to being part of the problem, and then, that done, just keep your mouth shut.

In the second place, Ducavalier continued his exposition in Sarajevo as he crushed out the cigarette held in his elegant fingers with yellow fingernails, the left had shamelessly thrown itself into the arms of neo-liberalism and betrayed the working class by declaring the concept of the class struggle obsolete, an attempt to deny the existence of those they were supposed to be protecting, since there are still more than enough people in our societies for whom belonging to the working class is simply a reality—it's no wonder, he added, that those parties that are at least willing to admit that the struggle isn't over are experiencing a boom right now, even if they systematically and deliberately identify the wrong adversary. The first signs of this betrayal were already evident in the '80s under Mitterrand, then in the '90s in Clinton's America, followed by Tony Blair, that midget, and his despicable German sidekick, Schröder.

Here Kraft had to contradict him, didn't Schröder and his reforms put German industry back on solid footing and isn't Germany in such a strong position today because of him? Oh, Schröder . . . Ducavalier exclaimed, don't start in with the Agenda 2010. Treason, it was treason, and just look at the state of social democracy in Germany today! They had all drunk a great deal, their discussion progressed in broad strokes, the details becoming increasingly scarce in the alcohol-induced haze. I'll tell you how things were with Schröder, Bertrand grumbled, a fresh cigarette between his lips: the moment he became chancellor, he realized there were others who had even more power, the people in the upper echelons of Deutsche Bank, the chief executives at Siemens, Porsche, and Thyssen-Krupp, and above all, they had more money. Poor Gerhard couldn't stand it, he suddenly felt very small, so he cozied up to them, so that they'd at least include him in their arrogant jockeying to show who's got the biggest balls. No, I'm telling you, Bertrand announced confidently, for an entire generation of Germans, Schröder is the political disappointment of their lives. Imagine, you grow up in Germany and all you know is Kohl— sixteen years of Kohl. But don't try to tell me, Kraft, my friend, that you wouldn't have suffered. Sixteen years of shame and anguish and then comes Schröder and it's as if someone finally opened a window and let in some fresh air. Then he betrayed them, all of them . . . the

Genosse der Bosse, the bosses' comrade, a nickname that, thanks to Ducavalier's German, nurtured by his reading of Husserl, and his French accent, expressed the deepest disgust. The greatest disappointment of their political lives, for an entire generation. I don't understand, he exclaimed, why no one assassinated him . . . they're not angry enough, these young people . . . someone should have cut his throat, and Ducavalier flailed a butter knife through the cigarette smoke to illustrate his point.

He wasn't entirely wrong, Kraft felt, because Schröder was a difficult figure for him too. Of course, it had been disconcerting that it was a social democrat, of all people, who had, so to speak, pulled the revered count's plan from the desk drawer to which Kohl had relegated it after wholeheartedly trumpeting an intellectual and moral turn, but Kraft could ultimately accept this. What weighed more heavily on him was that the kind of thinking with which he and his sidekick István were once able to send their fellow students into a rage had, in fact, as Bertrand claimed, shifted over the years to become centrist and then even farther to the left. Kraft had lost his distinguishing characteristic. His opinions were no longer remarkable among his fellow social scientists. To be sure, there still weren't many who openly expressed their views as economic liberals, but when Kraft did so, it was as if he were publicly admitting to consuming pornography—it was, in other words, a completely superfluous admission: no one was ashamed of consuming pornography any longer, but, really, there was no need to talk about it.

The precipitous fall of the center-right, economic-liberal Free Democratic Party was another source of anguish for Kraft—seeing the party leadership devolving upon one ridiculous figure after another until, at some point, the helm was taken by two lads who reminded Kraft uncomfortably of István and himself in younger years and steered the once proud party into irrelevance. Even Dr. Hamm-Brücher had had enough after forty-five years and quit. She resigned her membership on the very day the twins were born and Kraft felt strangely affected.

No, for some time now there been no joy for Kraft in waving the banner of freedom or lending his voice to the song of privatization through deregulation or to the chorus of praise for the rainmakers . . .

ⓐ nd how are you planning on defending optimism? Kraft asks Bertrand. I'm not, Ducavalier says with a laugh, and taps a cigarette from the pack. He will do the opposite. He has come as a prophet of doom. Someone had to play the role, and he's the perfect man for the job. For most of the people delivering papers here, a million dollars is simply too large a sum of money—you can't blame them for going about the thing pragmatically. He, however, can afford to play the dissident and forgo the million.

That will be my sacrifice, and as you can see, my dear Richard, it will hardly be a real one. That is the bane of my existence: I never can manage to make a legitimate sacrifice.

What he plans to do, Ducavalier tells Kraft, is to take on the task of explaining why almost everything that is, is bad. A rather easy task, he adds, and gives a brief overview of the coming apocalypse: the impending collapse of the European Union; the return of nationalism; the new acceptability of open racism and bigotry; the democratically elected despots who turn their countries into dictatorships with their peoples' consent—a process that makes one doubt the usefulness of democracy itself; the rising tide of anti-intellectualism, for which the intellectuals themselves are responsible, and the accompanying legitimation of ignorance; the openly expressed longing for strongmen;

the moral bankruptcy of the economic elite who behave like unrepentant secondhand-car dealers; the threat of a new economic crisis against which the central banks will be left with no possible recourse, since they can't devalue money any more than they already have, as a consequence of which they've already shot the last arrow in their quiver; a free trade policy combined with a protectionist system of subsidies that drives millions of poor people from the south to the north; the stagnation of economic growth despite the digital revolution; the lack of alternatives to capitalism even though capitalism leads inevitably to an ever greater disparity in wealth that will in turn cut the system's legs out from under it in the near future; the millions of surplus young men in China and India who are badly educated, sexually frustrated, and without hope of a future, a problem that will be most elegantly solved with a war of aggression . . . And, although he is of course aware that it is an unacceptable if terribly effective simplification, he will give his explanation theoretical and narrative weight by using a cyclical philosophy of history that will allow him to evoke in his conclusion a return of the conditions that existed during the Weimar Republic, thus conjuring a third world war that will hover implacably over the assembly. *Et voilà*, Bertrand says . . . all that is, is bad.

Kraft pulls a lettuce leaf from his ham sandwich. You forgot climate change, he says to Ducavalier.

Eighteen minutes, my dear Kraft, you've got to set some limits. Eighteen minutes is not enough to describe the world's depravity in full.

Kraft uses the hours remaining before the conference to tinker with his PowerPoint presentation. Pragmatically, but cheerlessly, he inserts one bullet point after another: God, who created the best possible world, the necessity of evil, the weaknesses of the individual that guarantee the cohesion of the Great Chain of Being, the elegance of the whole system—writing this, he thinks of Herb, whom he had denigrated as an apostle of the system and whose cocoa he drank so gratefully. Kraft is but a shadow of himself at this point, he's had to eat a lot of crow on this trip. Now he can see it all through to the end and thus definitively turn his back on himself. And so he launches into a point-by-point misuse of Vogl's oikodicy, then begins to praise technology until his systematizing leads him to the technological Singularity. And suddenly he understands why Erkner feels such longing for that moment and it now seems perfectly logical to Kraft that artificial intelligence should become man's equal and then surpass him, which will entail a rapid acceleration of technological development in a direction no one is now in a position to depict and a merging of man and machine, thanks to which man will be able leave behind his biologically limited existence and exist in timeless substrate.

All narrow-minded objections critical of modernity shrivel to the status of dejected nitpicking in the face of this vision's redemptive dimensions. To be sure, at the moment AI can't even tell the difference between a picture of Nicki Minaj's behind and the real thing, but isn't that the wrong way to look at it? . . . a typical European objection . . . indulging in pessimistic pettiness instead of recognizing all that is already possible, how quickly progress is being made, how the recently unthinkable already appears mundane, and if you add in exponential development, don't we have legitimate grounds to extrapolate such fantastic expectations?

No, Kraft doesn't want to resist any longer, the Singularity is unavoidable and now that he's accepted this, he also understands that, faced with the dimensions of the coming change, there's no point in regretting that everything he knows, his entire world—material and nonmaterial—will go the way of film and vinyl records and at best survive merely as the eccentric hobby of men spoiled by affluence. And his own fears are just as insignificant, because they are centered on irrelevant categories. Machines that are superior to man in intelligence, apocalypticists warn us, will treat us as slaves or a source of food, at best as pets . . . That's nonsense. As if concepts from the old order would play any role whatsoever in that new world.

Our man Kraft has the feeling that seeing things from this perspective relieves him of a heavy burden. He's overcome by a feeling of purity he knows only from that rare and precious daydream in which the ultimate truth appears to him as a piece of silver, gleaming like a mirror and as hard as diamond. But now he knows that he won't have to lay that truth bare by scraping away with argument after argument, with merciless reflection, all the rotting organic dross and excrement that cling to it. No, this silver thing waits at the end of history, because history—it is now entirely clear to him—will come to an end and a new history will begin, a history in which humans can watch, from the comfort of the passenger seat of evolution, where the journey leads. Whether he is a fox, hedgehog, or porcupine, man will be able to be whatever he wants and he will want to be something that we, at present, cannot even imagine.

For a while, Kraft searches for a fitting image with which he can conclude his presentation. He clicks through pictures of sunrises and lights at the end of tunnels, gets lost in NASA's photo archive amid images of launching rockets and the nebulae in distant galaxies, and finally decides on a photograph of the Blue Grotto of Capri, in the center of which a smooth, white expanse of light dispels the darkness.

He skips the early-evening reception in the courtyard of the Hoover Institution where Erkner welcomes the conference participants.

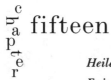

fifteen

Heile, heile Gänsje
Es is bald widder gut,
Es Kätzje hat e Schwänzje
Es is bald widder gut,
Heile heile Mausespeck
In hunnerd Jahr is alles weg.

Don't cry my little gosling
All will be well again,
The cat has got its tail
All will be well again,
You will have your candy, my little mouse
In a hundred years it will all be gone.

—GERMAN NURSERY RHYME

ow, finally, Kraft knows what he has to do. It doesn't come in a flash, but rather as his recognizing a possibility that has accompanied him for a long time, perhaps his entire life. On this sleepless night, in the burning shame that fills him from head to toe at the thought of Johanna, of Heike, of the unspeakable PowerPoint presentation that, he fears, will win him points with Erkner and send him home with a million dollars, this possibility has ripened into a certainty and needs only to be put into action. A fox is no hedgehog and is no porcupine either.

Kraft sits at the desk in the dark, opens his laptop, and begins systematically erasing all traces of the work he's done over the past few days. He empties his backpack of everything except his notes. Then he puts on his lightweight suit, polishes the tips of his shoes with a sock, and slips his new smartphone into his pocket. He carries his shoes in his hand, shoulders his backpack, and creeps through the sleeping house and down the stairs. Ivan's keys are in a glass bowl in the foyer. Kraft grabs them and crosses the kitchen to the garage. He finds what he's looking for in moments. He had noticed the rope on the shelf a few days earlier and for a long time now, Kraft has been making mental notes of every rope he sees lying about.

He sits on the steps in front of the house and puts on his shoes. He throws his notes in the paper-recycling bin in the driveway across the street. The streets are empty and the heels of his Budapesters echo loudly through the mild night. Kraft walks quickly. A light still burns in a laboratory building. He passes a jogging student who nods at him breathlessly.

The tower of books rises crudely into the night sky. Lights shine on the four corners of the observation deck. He opens the door with Ivan's key. An EMERGENCY EXIT sign weakly illuminates the lobby of the Hoover Institution on War, Revolution, and Peace. The elevator is out of order, so he takes the stairs. He gropes his way in the dark until he remembers he can use the flashlight on his phone. Kraft pushes open the door to the observation deck. He briefly stands in one of the grilled niches. The lights of Silicon Valley twinkle at his feet. In the distance, San Francisco disappears into the fog. Then he turns toward the carillon. The small glass cubicle with the keyboard and above it the bells amid the dark roof beams. He climbs arduously onto the glass cubicle. The panes give his leather soles no purchase, he has to take off his socks and shoes. A grille blocks his way to the bells but he manages to bend it without making too much noise. Then he puts his socks and shoes back on, polishing the tips once more with the ball of his hand. From there, he easily climbs higher onto the beams. He takes the rope from his backpack. A faint smell of mortadella reaches his nose, but that doesn't stop him. Kraft knows how to tie a proper knot. He carefully tests the length and ties the other end onto the clapper of the largest bell. He opens the Famethrower app that one of the engineers installed for him. He connects it to a live-stream app and starts broadcasting. He props the telephone at the right height on a beam. Kraft puts the noose around his neck and checks the screen. No one is watching. He waits. A user in Bogotá connects.

—Hola, qué pasa!

No Famestars. But no Wrinkles either. Kraft waits. Bogotá soon disconnects. Kraft tests the knot and waits. Then he has a viewer from Turkey and soon one from Finland. Then Greg from Winnipeg connects as well. Greg is concerned.

—Hey dude, don't do whatever you plan to do! Where are you? Should I call somebody? Dude . . . she is not worth it!!!!

Finland disconnects. Kraft waits. He's no Justin Bieber, Kraft knows that. But there should be at least five or six. Greg insists:

—Don't do it, man!!! I promise, whatever it is, it will be all right.

Kraft lets himself fall into the void. His neck breaks with the reliable sound Bakelite hair clippers make when they're turned on. The bell begins to swing. The clapper hits. Kraft no longer hears it. *For Peace Alone Do I Ring.*

acknowledgments

The ETH Zürich Foundation made it possible for me to spend three years working on a dissertation in philosophy. Unfortunately, nothing came of that dissertation, though some of the material I reflected on in my academic work has found its way into the novel at hand. I would like to thank Michael Hampe and my former colleagues in the Chair for Philosophy for the stimulating environment.

The Swiss National Foundation granted me a nine-month stipend to conduct research at Stanford University, where I wrote the first sketches of *Kraft*. Sepp Gumbrecht was a wonderful host at the Department of Comparative Literature and I am grateful for my many discussions with him and others, in particular Adrian Daub, who has thought deeply about the culture of Silicon Valley, and Amir Eshel, in whose seminars we wrestled with Job and the theodicy.

I must apologize to the aforementioned for abandoning my dissertation. I am holding out the faint hope that for one or another of them this novel will offer some compensation.

By presenting me with a sabbatical year, the city of Zürich eased my decision to dedicate myself completely to writing.

Odo Marquand's essays were pivotal when I began my engagement with theodicy. Marion Hellwig's study *Alles ist gut* ("Everything Is Right"; Würzburg, 2008) was a great help during the writing of this book. Along with the classic works, Hans Poser's essay "Von der Theodizee zur Technodizee: Ein altes Problem in neuer Gestalt" ("From Theodicy to Technodicy: An Old Problem in a New Guise"; Hannover, 2011) and Joseph Vogl's *Das Gespenst des Kapitals* ("The Specter of Capitalism"; Zürich, 2010/11) were particularly important.

I would like to thank Ulrike Arnold and Stefan Willer for their careful readings of the manuscript and for their countless comments. I also thank my agent Karin Graf for accompanying me in this endeavor.

My thanks also extend to everyone who worked with me at Publishers C.H. Beck, especially Martin Hielscher, and to Maximilian Häusler for his assistance with my research.

And I thank my friend Michael Zichy for his constant willingness to discuss the evil in the world in all its facets.

sources

CHAPTER ONE

Ford, Paul. "The Message," *Medium*, August 13, 2014, at http://medium.com/s /story/how-to-be-polite-9bf1e69e888c.

CHAPTER TWO

Thiess, Richard. *Ladendiebstahl erkennen, verhindern, verfolgen: Ein Handbuch für die Praxis.* Marburg: Tectum, 2011, p. 18. Excerpt translated by Tess Lewis.

CHAPTER THREE

King James Bible, Job 40:16–17.

CHAPTER FOUR

Balzac, Honoré de. *Histoire des treize: La Duchesse de Langeais*, 1834. Excerpt translated by Tess Lewis.

CHAPTER FIVE

Voltaire. *Candide, ou l'optimisme*, 1759. Excerpt translated by Tess Lewis.

CHAPTER SIX

Flach, Karl-Hermann, Werner Maihofer, and Walter Scheel. *Die Freiburger Thesen der Liberalen*. Rheinbeck: Rowohlt, 1972, p. 61. Excerpt translated by Tess Lewis.

CHAPTER SEVEN

From *The Martian*, 2015. Twentieth Century Fox. Written by Drew Goddard.

CHAPTER EIGHT

Hamm-Brücher, Hildegard. *Untersuchungen an den Hefemutterlaugen der technischen Ergosterin-Gewinning*. Dissertation at the University of Munich, 1945, p. 94. Excerpt translated by Tess Lewis.

CHAPTER NINE

Lichtenberg, Georg Christoph. *Sudelbücher J* 166. Excerpt translated by Tess Lewis.

CHAPTER TEN

Ford Sakaguchi. *Riding History: Sketches on Shifting Presences and Converging Horizons*. Lands End: Huntington University Press, 1992, p. 69.
Cowtan, Gary. Lyrics to "Looking for Freedom." Originally sung by Marc Seaburg, as produced by Jack White. David Hasselhoff's recording of the song dates from 1989.

CHAPTER ELEVEN

Marquard, Odo. *Individuum und Gewaltenteilung: Philosophische Studien*. Ditzingen: Reclam, 2004, p. 126. Excerpt translated by Tess Lewis.

CHAPTER TWELVE

Schelling, Friedrich Wilhelm Joseph von. Quoted in Goethe, Johann Wolfgang von, *Begegnungen und Gespräche: 1800–1805*, Renate and Ernst Grumach, eds. Berlin: Walter de Gruyter, 1985, p. 142. Excerpt translated by Tess Lewis.

CHAPTER THIRTEEN

Metastasio, Pietro. *Didone abbandonata*, 1794. Act I, Scene 13.

CHAPTER FOURTEEN

Hoover, Herbert. Quoted in Leuchtenburg, William E., *Herbert Hoover*. The American Presidents Series: The 31st President, 1929–1933. New York: Times Books, 2009, p. 17.